BEGINNINGS

BEGINNINGS

THE WIZARD AND THE WARRIOR
BOOK ONE

Vivienne Lee Fraser

www.viviennelfraser.com.au

Vivienne Lee Fraser
www.viviennelfraser.com.au

Cataloguing-in-Publication details are available
from the National Library of Australia
www.trove.nla.gov.au
ISBN: 978-0-6482181-0-4

Formatting and cover design by KILA Designs
www.kiladesigns.com.au
Cover image: ©bigstockphoto.com

Illustrations provided by Anna Bazel
www.fiverr.com/annabazyl

*For Harry Williamson, who always said
I should be a writer. Finally, Granddad.*

*And for Jim and Sam who have
supported me while I gave my dream a go.*

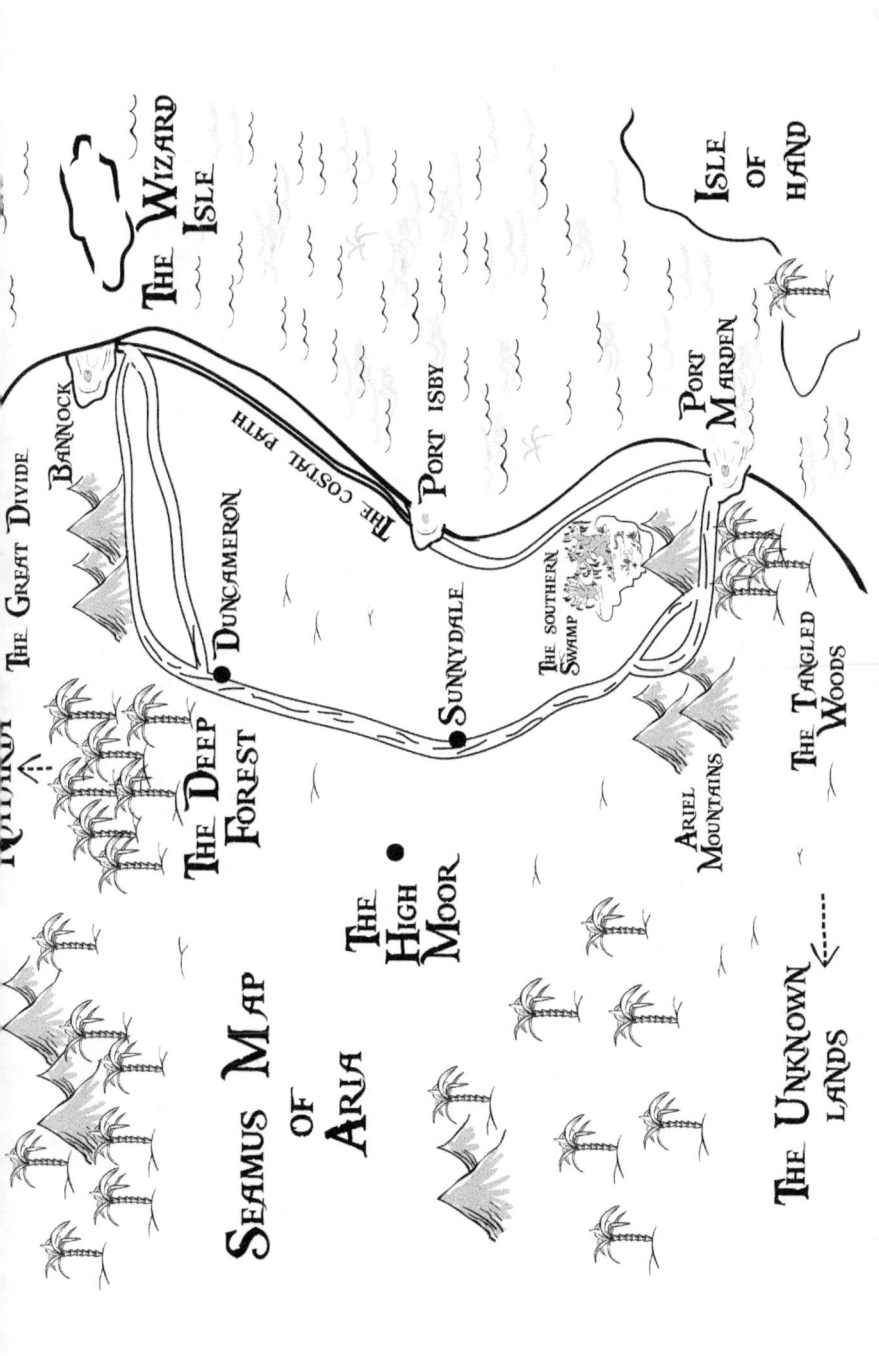

PROLOGUE

When the new power rises and the
Wizard and Warrior meet, old and new blood
will combine to save one and all.

The elderly man gazed into the fire, his eyes drawn to the ship he watched leaving Bannock Harbour. He continued to watch until it was well on its way out to sea, then rose slowly, rubbing his aching back. 'So it begins,' he thought to himself. 'And a good thing too, as there is none with the skill to follow me as High Seer. So none but I have the learning to pass on to the Wizard and Warrior that they will need to defeat their enemy. I just hope they make it here in good time.'

He looked up as his apprentice opened the door. 'Eon, please advise the Council I need to be heard.'

'The signs were correct? It is time?' his apprentice asked, his eyes gleaming with excitement.

'Yes,' the Seer said with less enthusiasm. 'It is time. Come now, we have much to do and little time in which to do it.'

1

1
ESCAPE

Aliah counted slowly to twenty before she slipped off the bed and tiptoed to the door, reluctantly passing the bread and cheese the boy had left on the wooden table in the middle of her cabin. Her hunger would have to wait. The ship rolled as she neared the door, throwing her off-balance and hip-first into the table. Biting back a yelp, she waited for another count of twenty to see if anyone heard the bang before trying the door handle.

The boy had been getting lazy and these last few days

had not locked the door in between bringing her food and taking the empty plates away. Fortunately he had not changed his habits even though they were in port. Perhaps the excitement of being able to leave the ship after a six day at sea had prevented him from realising the opportunity he had presented to his captain's valuable cargo.

Looking down the corridor the only hint of other people on board was the hustle and bustle of sailors working on deck. She quickly grabbed her cloak off the sea chest and put it on. Then, without a moment to lose, continued her silent exit from the cabin that had been her prison for the last four days.

Hesitating for a moment at the end of the corridor, she peeked around the corner to see if there was anyone in the galley before darting quickly past the entrance. She halted again by some barrels near the foredeck stairs. Did she have a better chance of escape by heading up the stairs and hoping that everyone was too busy unloading cargo to notice her? Or was she best to try and stow away in the cargo hold and hope to be unloaded? No, too many sailors would be working there, she might be spotted. Best she take her chances in amongst the cargo on deck.

Aliah crept up the stairs on hands and knees. At the top, she stuck her head above the opening to get an idea of her next move. Ducking quickly back into the shadows at the side, she held her breath as footsteps approached hoping no one had seen her. The footsteps passed and she slowly let out her breath. Taking another look, she confirmed there was a stack of barrels about ten paces away, which were about another ten paces from the gangplank. If she could make it to the barrels she might be able to blend in with the sailors carrying cargo to the dock. She looked down at her blue gown and dainty white shoes; well, maybe if she weren't dressed for attending a state dinner.

Quickly, she crawled back down the stairs and moved aft towards the crew quarters. The ship boy was about her size. Surely she could find something to wear from his clothes. The sound of singing ahead halted her progress and she tried the door behind her.

Fortunately it was open and she slipped silently inside just before the cook passed on his way back to the galley. Luck must really have been on Aliah's side as she had stumbled into the first mate's cabin and he must have come in earlier to lay out clean clothes for shore leave. Even more fortunately he was not a tall man.

Aliah managed to change quickly, tucking in the rough shirt and rolling the trousers to fit.

There were no socks to wear with the boots under the bed so she tore her petticoats and wrapped bandages around her feet. With her make-do footwear the boots were considerably more snug on her feet. She then tucked her plait of blonde hair down the back collar of the shirt to ensure it would not get in the way, or immediately alert anyone to the fact she was a girl. She grabbed his spare cap and jammed it onto her head. Finally she laid out her own clothing on the bed as a bit of a joke, chuckling to herself as she imagined the first mate actually wearing her dress. 'Ready?' Taking a deep breath she moved to leave, then stopped.

There, behind the door, was her sword still in its scabbard with its blue jewelled hilt sticking out the top. She quickly grabbed one of her most prized possessions and tied its belt around her waist. Catching sight of her cloak she decided to take it with her, and swung it over her shoulders. Who knew what it might come in handy for?

Just as she was ready to leave, the door of the cabin began to open. Ducking in behind it she cursed herself for leaving her dress in full view on the bed. Well, it was too late now. The first mate started to enter the room then stopped. He must have spotted the dress.

'Sound the alarm!' The door crashed closed as he ran out yelling for all to hear. From her position behind the door she could hear footsteps run down the hall and then the door opened again. Aliah was crushed against the wall as the first mate showed his bed to someone.

'She's only gone and blimmin stolen my clothes,' He complained to whoever he was showing her dress to.

'Well, you had best tell the captain,' the cook told him. 'Rather you than me.' He chuckled as he walked away.

The door closed again and Aliah let her breath slowly out. What should she do now? They would surely be on the lookout for her. She had to try and get off the ship. She may not get another chance before they reached their final destination. Aliah made it back to the stairs with no further mishaps, and silently crawled back into position on the second to last tread listening to see what was now happening on deck.

'But, Captain, we should search for her.' Near the opening the first mate was pleading with the captain.

'The men are busy loading and unloading cargo, Jenkins. That is where our real money is. We are not being paid enough for delivering her to make me change that.

BEGINNINGS

Besides, she can only get off the ship down a gangplank and we can see it from here. We will have plenty of time to stop her if she tries anything, and if she doesn't, then we can search for her when we are back at sea.' Turning away, the captain watched as his men hauled another load of cargo up from the hold.

'And, Jenkins, get some men to move those.' He pointed to the barrels Aliah had been planning to use for cover. 'We need to have them off now. I don't care if the fellow what paid for them is not ready to pick them up yet. I want to be off at the turn of the tide regardless,' The captain blustered.

'But, sir, if we unload them onto the docks they are bound to go missing. And the chap what bought them, he only paid us half up front. Can't see him paying up what's owed if he can't get his wine,' argued the first mate.

'Well ... well send the boy to see if he can't find him hanging around the docks,' countered the captain.

'I've already sent him looking for that blasted girl, sir.'

'Of course you have. Can't wait 'til we be rid of her next stop. Well, you have your orders Jenkins, I've got to check in with the quartermaster. Only two candle-marks 'til the tide turns and I want to be off then. Cannot make any money waiting round here!'

The captain strode off, but the first mate did not move away. He stood there mumbling about stolen clothes and grumping about not getting shore leave. Holding her breath she willed him to go about his business. In spite of her mental urgings he stood there for what seemed like an eternity muttering under his breath until, finally, he shouted, 'Hey, boy,' and his boots made a clipping sound on the deck as he walked away to do as the captain bid.

Aliah popped her head above deck level. As luck would have it, apart from the first mate talking to the ship's boy there was no one else on deck. 'It's now or never.' She launched herself towards the gangplank, deciding at the last minute to throw away her previous plan and make a full break for it.

Running as fast as her legs would carry her Aliah dashed for the gangplank, and was halfway down it before an astonished Jenkins yelled, 'Hey. *Hey*. Stop her.'

Just at that very moment a sailor carrying a sack of flour over each shoulder stepped onto the gangplank right in front of Aliah. '*Stop*,' yelled the first mate. The sailor in front of Aliah hesitated for a moment, undecided whether to look after the flour sacks on his shoulder or grab her. Aliah took her chances, dodging left then right past the large man, and leaping the last few steps onto the wharf.

Another sailor following his fellow crewmate grabbed her cloak and threw her to the ground. He tried to hold her down, but Aliah kicked out hitting his arm and rolled away. Scrabbling to her feet she faced the two sailors. They walked towards her and as she backed away she looked for something, anything, to help her. There was nothing. She drew her sword and swung at the arm of the man on the right. He was not quick enough to move away and the blade made an angry red slash down his arm. He took a step back to examine the damage.

'You'll pay for that girl!' The other sailor growled as he went to grab her. But Aliah's training had been thorough and as he moved forward she swung back around and

BEGINNINGS

he had a matching slash on his arm. Using her momentum she dodged through the gap between the two injured men and began running towards the warehouses at the far end of the harbour.

Standing on her bed as they had entered the harbour, Aliah had seen the warehouses at the end of the docks through her cabin porthole. Beyond that, she could just make out the buildings of the main town. It was towards those warehouses she headed now, hoping to make it to the town and get herself lost in the crowds. Weaving in and out of the hustle and bustle of the docks her captors struggled to catch up to her.

Three other ships were in port so there were plenty people working and milling around. Some were loading and unloading cargo, others were chatting to sailors, and there were a few passengers with their luggage waiting to be helped aboard. With so many people it was easy for Aliah to evade her pursuers. Ducking behind one of the carts Aliah found herself face to face with the first mate.

'Thought you could get away from me you little sneak thief?' Snarling, he made a grab for her. There was no room for her to use her sword, so she went limp as he grabbed her cloak. Believing he had the best of her, Jenkins pulled the girl in close. That was what she had been waiting for. With all her force she brought her knee up and Jenkins fell to the ground, his face a picture of pain. But he still held her cloak.

A shout from behind told her they had been spotted, so she quickly undid the cloak and dropped it over the first mate. Sheathing her sword she took off again through the crowd. When she was sure her pursuers could no longer see her, she slipped into a doorway of a warehouse and hunkered down behind what looked like—and certainly smelt like—bales of wool. It was as good as any place to hide until her captors tired of looking and returned to the ship to catch the turning tide.

What seemed like more than two candle marks later she could still hear sailors questioning people whether they had seen a boy in too large clothing, might even look a bit girl-like? But no, no one had seen anyone of that description. If the docks were not so busy they could have found her hiding place by following the noise of her rumbling stomach. If only she had taken the time to eat some of the midday meal that she had so casually crept passed earlier. Aliah stayed in her uncomfortable hiding spot trying not to notice how hungry she was and wondered how long it would be before she could actually leave.

Finally the sun started to set, and the docks quietened down. She crept from her hiding place, needing to move before the warehouse was locked for the night. Surely the ship would have left port by now and she would be safe to leave. Poking her head around the door she drew back quickly. The ship was still there. And what's more they had posted lookouts on the deck. She would be an easy target walking along the deserted docks.

'Yep, they still be looking for you lad.' Aliah swung round, coming face to face with a white bearded man sitting on a stool in the shadows on the other side of the door. 'They must want you something bad to miss the tide like that.'

Dumbfounded, Aliah just stared at the man with her

mouth open.

'Paid your parents for you did they? And you decided the sea not the life for you I s'pect.' The man nodded wisely at her, and Aliah nodded in return, too scared to actually tell him the truth. 'Ah, well.' The man rose from his stool, putting down the rope he was mending. 'You ain't the first and I s'pect you won't be the last, and it were many a long year ago I did the same.' He stretched out his back, then reached up and closed the warehouse door, leaving Aliah in the dark.

'Well, I best be heading home now. Out THE BACK DOOR, which is always open. Don't s'pose I would even notice if anyone went through it afore me.' He picked up his stool and rope, heading for the lean too beside the door.

Astonished, it was a moment before Aliah took the hint and headed to the opposite end of the warehouse. Fortunately most of the stock appeared to be wool bales as she caught her shins on them more than once in the half-light as she headed towards the back door. At the other end she began looking for a latch. Finally her fingers found what seemed to be a handle. She grabbed hold of it and pushed the door out, nearly falling into the alleyway.

A quick look both ways showed her it was deserted. Without further hesitation she ran up the paved street in the opposite direction from the docks hoping she was heading into the centre of town. It was glorious to be free after so long.

2
PORT MARDEN

Seamus had been coming to Port Marden two or three times a year with his parents for as long as he could remember. So he knew the town well. Unfortunately that meant many people in the town knew him too. For this reason he kept to the back streets as he wandered, hoping he would not be easily recognised.

As he got closer to the markets the cobbled streets widened and the houses were larger and more prosperous looking. While many were still made of stone, some had second stories added made of wood and plaster. Many of these overhung the street, making a rough sort of cover.

Where the back streets had been quiet, those around the market were busier. The number of people increased. They were mainly traders carrying their unsold goods home to their waiting families. He kept his cap down but nodded to people he passed so as not to seem unfriendly. If people thought him unfriendly they may remember him later, then his parents might hear he was wandering around by himself.

As he walked his mind ticked over. He needed time to himself because he needed to think. He needed to decide what to do. And he needed to decide soon because things were getting out of control.

'Things.' He laughed to himself. 'Me. I am getting out of control.'

Seamus replayed the scene from that afternoon in his head. When his brother had barged into his room to hide, Seamus' fright sent the books on his desk flying towards the opening door. Fortunately he lunged to the desk before his brother realised it had not been possible for him to throw the books from where he had been standing. From his brother's reaction he had managed to hide what had really happened. This time.

For the last few years those incidents had been increasing. The type of incidents where he could move things without touching them. In some areas of the country, like the Southern Duchy, having magic would be cause for celebration. But on the Island of Hand magic was forbidden.

So far he had managed to hide his growing talent, but recently there were more incidents where things had

BEGINNINGS

just happened as he thought them into being. He knew he could not go on the way things were. But what to do?

If he stayed on Hand he would have to undergo the process of quietening. His magic would be silenced forever. He was not sure he really wanted that. Magic was part of him. If he decided not to be quietened then he needed to leave and find someone to help him control his magic. Of course he could go to the school in the Wizard Isles and be trained as a full wizard. But that would mean never returning to Hand. What he really would like to do is find someone who could help him control and hide his magic so he could return home and no one would be any the wiser.

His wandering had brought Seamus close to the market square. Many of the buildings he passed were shops. Most of them were closing as their owners headed upstairs to spend the evening with their families. He stopped on the edge of the square. Directly across from him was The West Way, the main road out of Port Marden. It joined the main road along the coast towards the capital, Bannock. If he decided to leave at this time on a market day he should be able to blend in with the farmers and landowners leaving town. That way he would not be noticed by the guards.

The stallholders in the market were packing up and chatting to passers-by, trying to make a last minute sale so as not to have to carry their goods home. He would have to be careful as he went through as many of them might remember having seen him with his parents and would remember his being there. Then they would be able to tell those who came looking for him later that he had passed through. He needed some sort of disguise to blend in.

He decided to take a turn round the square before returning home. Startled by shouting, he stopped by a half-dismantled stall. At the bread stall across the way it looked as though the baker had taken pity on a boy and was giving him one of the loaves he had not sold that day. But that was not the cause of the disturbance. On the other side of the square were three sailors running and yelling at the boy—or maybe the baker—it was hard to tell which.

The boy looked towards the sailors, his eyes were wide with fear. The baker held on to the loaf and turned towards the sailors, his mouth open as if he was about to speak.

Seamus moved fast. He focused on the crates in front of the sailors, pointing to where he wanted them to be. They wobbled, then toppled with a loud crash and scattered across their path. The unsuspecting sailors tripped over the crates and fell to the ground in a tangle of arms and legs.

Seamus ran into the square, grabbed the boy's hand, and the loaf of bread, and started running towards The West Way. Dodging around carts and people they came face to face with another group of sailors. Seamus spun around, but the first group had untangled themselves and where coming up behind them. Out of the corner of his eye the baker was talking to two guards and pointing their way. Looking around and spotting a gap, he dragged the boy between two stalls then down the alley behind.

'Wait,' the boy gasped. 'We'll be trapped.'

BEGINNINGS

'Trust me.' Seamus pulled the boy through a line of washing, then ducked in behind a cart parked in the yard behind. He had often carried his mother's gowns here when she came to see the laundress.

Listening, he waited until the footsteps had passed, then pulled the boy back out the way they came and down the alley. As they entered the market, shouts from behind told him the sailors had spotted them and were back on the chase. He headed towards The West Way, running past the astonished guardsmen.

'Halt. Halt you there!'

Seamus had no intention of halting. He had used magic in public. He no longer had time to think about what to do in the future. The future was here, and it appeared it was time for him to leave Port Marden. He ran, pulling the boy behind him, until they joined the throng of farmers leaving the town after market day.

Now the best camouflage was to appear like everyone else, so he slowed down and took a quick look behind. He could not see anyone in pursuit. They ducked in behind a farmer's wagon for extra cover. Satisfied they now blended in with the crowd, he relaxed and started breathing normally.

'Can I have my hand back now?' A voice interrupted. 'I really am very hungry!'

Embarrassed, Seamus realised he still held the young boy's hand. He dropped it like a hot brick, and his face flushed red. Belatedly he also realised that he had no way of knowing whether the baker was indeed giving the bread to the boy, or taking it back because it had been stolen.

'Look here,' he said to the boy. 'I don't know what that

was all about, but I hope you haven't gotten me into any trouble. All I want is to get out of town.'

The boy frowned at him, and hitched the long bundle he was carrying in a blanket a bit closer. 'I did not ask you to help me! Anyway, I don't know why, but those sailors have been following me all day. Something about a boy who skipped ship. All I want is to get out of here and head home as well. Now I don't know if I can because the sailors might make trouble for me, and if I don't get home my family will be worried.' Seamus could see the boy's blue eyes were brimming with tears in the shadow of his cap.

Seamus bit his lip, thinking. 'If you promise you are not in any trouble, then I might be able to help. Maybe it might be an idea to team up for a bit?' He took a breath and continued. 'The sailors are looking for a boy by himself, and not two boys together. Us leaving together may confuse them for a while.' In his head he added, *And it will help me at the same time because my parents will be asking questions about a boy leaving town by himself as well.*

The boy looked at him skeptically then his blue eyes twinkling almost in mischief. 'Fine. But can I have my bread back? I have not eaten since I broke fast this morning.'

Seamus had entirely forgotten that he still held the loaf and rather sheepishly handed it over. The boy broke it in half and offered half back to Seamus, who took it and began to eat. He did not know when he would get a chance to buy food on his journey so he had best eat when he could.

BEGINNINGS

They shuffled with the crowd towards the gate in companionable silence, eating their bread and discretely looking about them for anyone following. Soon the traffic slowed almost to a halt as they approached the gate.

'What's going on?' Grumbled the woman behind them, trying to peer past. 'I have a long way to get home and these baskets aren't getting any lighter.'

'There's a hold-up at the gate,' came an answer from the farmer leading the cart in front of the boys. 'Guards must be checking for someone.'

Thinking fast Seamus shuffled so that he was beside the woman who had complained. She was carrying two baskets, one on top of the other, each half full of fruit or vegetables. Although her arms wrapped quite comfortably around the bottom basket, her head could barely see over the top.

'We sold all our goods today, perhaps we can help you carry yours for a while?' He tried his best to look like he genuinely wanted to help.

'You'll not be tricking me that easily young man,' the woman snapped back, her head looking around the baskets to glare at Seamus and his companion.

'I meant only to offer help,' Seamus said. 'Anyway, we could not run away with a basket in this crowd even if that was what we had planned. We are squeezed way too tight, and the guards would spot us. We have had a good day and I only meant to share our good luck.'

The woman looked with questioning brown eyes at Seamus, obviously still not quite sure whether to trust him. 'I am not certain you are telling the whole truth, but I believe your kindness may be genuine. I am sorry

I snapped young man, I am not used to people offering me help. If you and your brother would take the top basket for me, that would make my life a little easier.' Her back straightened a little as Seamus took the top basket down, then he and the boy took a handle each. Finally the other boy put his own strange bundle on top and they were ready to shuffle forward with the rest of the crowd.

Seamus adjusted his arm to account for the slightly shorter boy and they fell into pace beside the woman. She was dressed the same as many of the farm women at the market in a plain dark dress and her dark hair was caught beneath a scarf. At a guess Seamus thought she would be a little older than his own mother, and about the same height. Which meant she barely come up to his own shoulder. As she stared back at him, Seamus began talking as if he were with the woman.

'Your produce looks good,' he started. 'How come you are bringing so much home?'

'Mind your own business!' the woman snapped back. The look on Seamus' face must have softened her heart a little. 'Look, it's for reasons you best not know, young man. Carry that basket through the gates for me though, and you and your brother can fill your pocket's with whatever you can fit, for I do appreciate your help.'

'Thank you ma'am.' Seamus smiled his most charming smile. He only had the clothes on his back, his table knife, and a few coins in his pocket, so every penny he saved on food would make his journey a little easier.

BEGINNINGS

'What are your names?' the woman asked as they drew closer to the gate.

'Sean.' The boy who had saved her from the sailors said. 'Ali,' Aliah mumbled.

'I am Amelia.' The woman smiled for the first time. 'Now do you want to tell me why the guards up there are looking for one or both of you?' Amelia raised an eyebrow.

'Ah ...' Sean started, but Aliah rushed in whispering, 'It's me ma'am. I skipped ship today and some sailors have been looking for me.' When the old man in the warehouse had believed she was a boy jumping ship she had decided then and there that he had provided her with a great cover story, one that people in a port town would understand. So she ignored Sean's shocked look as he reacted to the fact she had lied to him less than a half candle-mark ago.

She had already tried her story out when she sold her cloak, her necklace, and the first mate's clothes and boots for something more her size. The owner of the second hand clothes stall had been sympathetic, saying that his nephew had been in a similar situation once. He could not do enough to help her, and had even offered to buy her sword, assuming it was stolen like the rest of her goods.

'No, thank you,' Aliah said as gruffly as she could. 'I might need it on the road home.' The stall owner had agreed that might be wise, and even given her a length of old blanket to wrap it in until she was safely out of town. Her story gained her some sympathy with the towns folk, so she was a little surprised at Amelia's response.

'Sorry, lad, it is not that I doubt your story, but the

duke's soldiers do not come out looking for a ship boy escaping his bond. You got a better tale young man? Best be quick as we are nearly at the gate.'

Aliah looked at Sean as he pulled his cap down lower on his head, almost hiding his nearly black eyes. She suddenly remembered the boxes that had moved seemingly by themselves in the market place. 'You,' she said. 'They're looking for you! Because of the boxes.'

'Boxes?' Amelia asked. 'What boxes?'

'He made the boxes move. In the marketplace,' Aliah blurted out and the boy on the other side of the basket turned red—not an easy task considering his dark complexion. It confirmed her suspicions, although he tried to pretend otherwise.

'Did not,' he mumbled.

Aliah did not know whether to be annoyed her escape might be thwarted by someone else running from the authorities, or relieved that the soldiers were not looking for her, or thankful he had saved her in the marketplace.

'Ah,' Amelia said. 'A budding wizard, that might be worth risking my hide for. Stay close by and let me do the talking. Then you can tell me the truth of the matter when we set camp for the night.'

Camp for the night? Aliah thought. *I shall be long gone by then.*

She and her companion fell in behind the woman as they approached the gate. 'Good evening to you,' Amelia said to the soldier who stopped them. 'We had little luck at the markets today and have a long walk home. Will you be keeping us much longer?'

'Have you seen a young man traveling by himself?' the

soldier asked. 'He would be about the age of your eldest, but in better clothes and a might more refined looking?'

'Can't say that I have,' Amelia answered. 'Mind you, it would be hard to tell in this crowd!'

'That it is,' the soldier responded. 'But we have orders to look anyway. I will need your boys to stand aside until the captain gets here. He needs to check all boys around a certain age. You can go through and wait for them on the other side.'

Amelia relieved them of their basket as Aliah and the boy Sean were grabbed roughly by the arm and pulled to the right of the gate where two other boys awaited the captain's visit.

'Next waiting.' The guard had already moved on and their new friend Amelia had no choice but to go through the gate.

'We can't wait here,' Sean whispered to her. He was gnawing at his lip.

'I don't see we have any choice,' Aliah whispered back.

Sean suddenly stopped chewing his lip and half-smiled. 'I think I have an idea. Play along.'

'Oww,' he groaned and doubled over. 'Oww, me stomach. I think I need a privy. Fast.'

Aliah bent over him looking concerned, then looked at the guard. 'Oh, dear. We have had the flux in our village. Looks like Sean might have it. Is there a privy near?'

The two guards looked at each other. Reluctantly the younger one moved towards them. 'Right, come this way. There is a privy in the guardroom. But be quick.'

He took them under the gate arch and showed them the door to the guard's rooms. 'Go up one flight and the privy is on the first floor. Be quick.'

Sean groaned again. 'We will, sir. And thank you.' Aliah grabbed Sean's arm and helped him through the door. They headed up the stairs. On the first landing she went to take him through as the guard had directed, but he stopped her.

'Keep going up,' he whispered.

Up two more flights of steep stairs they came out along the top of the gates. Checking to make sure there were no guards up there watching, Sean started crawling along the ramparts to the left side gate tower. Aliah followed. He led her into the other tower, down the steps to the ground floor and into an empty room. The room had a barred door through the outer wall.

'Help me with this,' Seamus ordered, and began to lift the bar. He gestured to Aliah to open the door while he held the wooden bar up. He then had her squeeze through the opening. When she was done he propped the bar with the haft of a spear that was beside the door, before lying down on the floor and wiggling through the small opening. Once on the other side, Seamus jolted the spear haft out of place and the bar fell down, closing the door with a bang.

'How did you know about that?' she asked Sean in amazement.

'My cousin and I have used it a couple of times. Although I don't remember it being such a tight squeeze,' he told her.

'Come on,' she said, urging him forward towards the stream of people on the main road. 'We need to be well clear of here when they realise we are not coming back from the guard room.'

BEGINNINGS

Watching the guards to make sure they were not spotted, Aliah and Sean joined the farmers leaving Port Marden for the night.

'Thought I might find you out here.'

Aliah jumped, startled to find Amelia standing behind them. 'But how ...?' Aliah frowned at the woman.

Amelia moved them through the crowd to the side of the road and she put down the baskets. Aliah realised the one she had been carrying still had her sword on top. It was a good thing Amelia had found them, as Aliah would not have liked to leave that behind.

'Do not worry. I will not tell them how you escaped. And I am as good as my word,' Amelia said to them. 'You can fill your pockets with fruit and vegetables and be on your way. But if you are smart you will help me with my baskets a little longer and we can plan your next moves. For as sure as I am standing here neither of you are prepared to journey far from here, and that is certainly what both of you intend to do.'

Aliah could tell Sean was considering the proposal, and she took some time to think it through herself. Given that it was nearly dark she really had nothing to lose by spending the night with these strangers, and it may turn out to her benefit.

'What exactly are you suggesting?' Sean asked.

'My place is on the edge of the Tangled Woods, which is a little under a half days walk from here. When I travel to market I leave some food in a spot not far off so I can stop for the night if it gets too late for traveling. If you carry my baskets that far, I can make you supper and we can sleep the night round a fire.'

Vivienne Lee Fraser

'But I want to go north,' Aliah protested, thinking maybe staying with the rather strange woman was not such a good idea after all. 'The Tangled Woods are west of here, I would lose valuable time.'

'You will not be able to travel much farther tonight and I would not mind betting that your sailor friends know you will be heading north. They will be expecting you to go home. If you wait the night through and set off tomorrow you might actually be doing yourself a favour. If you were prepared to wait a day or two more I have no doubt your journey would be even safer.' Amelia grinned at her, her warm brown eyes crinkling at the corners.

Aliah pondered this for a moment, then nodded in agreement. There was a lot of sense in Amelia's words. If she took tonight to get some warm food in her stomach, she might just avoid her pursuers and start out fresh in the morning.

'And what about you young man?' Amelia looked at Sean.

'I might as well be on my way,' he answered curtly.

'I see you have not thought this through either.' Amelia stared intently at Sean. 'Your pursuers will know you are headed for the Wizard Isles and on the road north. Once they do not find you at the gate, they will head along the Great North Road looking for you. They will have horses and you will be walking. You will be easily found.

'Add to that the fact that you are not prepared for any sort of journey. No food. No bedroll. No idea, really. It may be best for you that those looking for you find you.'

'Why should you care?' Sean blurted, clearly not happy about the flaws in his plan being pointed out by a woman he had just met.

Amelia laughed. 'Fair question, and I have to say I am asking myself that very thing. Normally I would not bother, but it has been a while since anyone showed me any kindness, even if it was for their own ends. So I find I am quite well disposed towards the both of you at the moment.

'Maybe I am also thinking I may be able to talk you out of the roads you are following. I sense your journeys will bring you great troubles, and I would not wish those troubles on anyone, especially two as unprepared for travel as the both of you.

'However, the offer is not good for long as I am not generally a woman to take to strangers. Either you come with me now, or you don't. I won't press you either way.' Amelia picked up her basket, making it clear she wanted to be on her way.

Aliah did not need any more encouragement. She would like a good nights sleep and some warm food before starting her journey home. Picking up the handle of her basket she looked at Sean. He seemed to be having a harder time deciding what to do. Finally he bent down and grabbed the handle on his side and they followed Amelia on the path towards the Tangled Woods.

Seamus walked behind the strange woman in silence. He was still not sure he had made the right decision and, if he admitted it to himself, he was a little annoyed at Amelia for pointing out how ill prepared he was for his journey. His departure had been a last minute decision. So not only did he not have the basics he needed to survive travelling, he also had no real plan of where he was going.

He knew he was nowhere near as prepared as he needed to be, but he did not need anyone pointing that out to him. And on top of it all, that boy, Ali, had lied to him about who he was, and now he was stuck traveling with him. It was definitely not how he would have planned to leave home. Still, he was happy to let people think he was heading towards the Wizard Isles. Maybe he would go there. Now he had shown he had magic in public it was not like he would be able to go home again.

By the time Amelia reached the copse of trees where she had left her pack, the last of the days light was almost gone and the air was getting decidedly chilly. Seamus was feeling more than a little tired and grumpy, and really annoyed that he had lost his home because he tried to help a boy who ended up being a liar.

'Put the baskets down there boys, then rummage around and see what wood you can find for a fire. Looks like it will be a might cold tonight.' Amelia busied herself with pulling what she needed for an evening meal out of the pack she had stowed behind a tree.

Sean and Ali put their basket down beside Amelia's and they both went into the copse to find wood before it got too dark to see. By the time they had finished, Amelia had started a small fire and set up a cooking billy. She cut up some of the vegetables from her basket into it, and poured a little water from a water skin she retrieved from her pack. She used the last of the water then handed it to Seamus.

'Just on the other side of the copse is a stream, we will be needing more water.'

BEGINNINGS

Seamus stopped himself from asking why he had to do it, appreciating it might seem odd for him to expect others to do the menial work. Taking the water skin, he hurried back into the copse and quickly found the stream. By the time he headed back to the fire it was almost pitch black and he was grateful for the light to guide him.

'Thank you young man.' Amelia took the water skin, poured some in the pot, and drank some from the skin. She then passed it to Ali, who passed it back to him so they could all drink something after their walk.

'The evening meal should be a few minutes more. Why don't you make yourself comfortable?'

Seamus sat down beside Ali. It seemed his task had been to find a suitable log for a back rest, which Seamus appreciated as he leaned back and relaxed, letting some of the tension go from his shoulders. He took off his cap, placing it on the log beside him, then ran his hand through his unruly black hair. Closing his eyes while he warmed up and waited for dinner the rest of his grumpy mood disappeared. He was even feeling a little less grumpy with the boy Ali. After all, the boy had not actually asked for his help. It could not be easy being sold to work on a ship by your family.

He wondered what his family would be doing now. Had they returned to the Isle of Hand and left the search for him up to the soldiers? Or had they stayed in their house in Port Marden? Had they heard about him using magic? Were they disappointed? He had not realised he dozed off until he felt Ali's hand shaking him awake.

The stew of grains and vegetables Amelia had made was nourishing and surprisingly tasty as she had added some herbs from a pouch in her bag. Once they had eaten their fill she cleaned the billy out while Ali cleaned their plates. Amelia then started to brew a tea for them from a collection of herbs from yet another pouch she had stowed.

It seems like she is well prepared, Seamus thought to himself.

'Now my boys, time for some planning before you both fall asleep.' She spoke as she threw some herbs into the boiling water, took the billy off the fire, and left the tea to steep.

'Let's start with you my young wizard. You are headed for the Wizard Isles to see if they will train you, are you not?' Amelia asked. Seamus nodded, as it seemed it was now his plan. 'So you have your family's permission in writing?'

Seamus sat up, no longer sleepy. 'No, what do you mean?'

'You do know they will not take a wizard to train without the family's permission, don't you? They do not want trouble, and so to prevent any misunderstandings they make sure the family agrees to training before they take a boy on.'

Seamus had not known that. Training to be a wizard was not something very much discussed in his family. He thought about how that changed what he was doing, and concluded it didn't. If the wizards would not take him then he would find someone else to teach him. Besides, he rather suspected that, given who he was, the wizards would welcome him with open arms.

'My family are of the old blood,' he told Amelia. 'To them a person able to wield magic is an abomination. They will have me quietened if I stay, and if I do not agree they will kill me. Surely the wizards will take pity on me and agree to train me without my parent's consent?' He felt like he was almost pleading with Amelia to believe him.

Amelia's face had gone very still and he could not read what she was thinking. 'You are old enough to have your marque?' she asked almost in a whisper. Seamus pulled up his sleeve and showed her the tattoo on the inside of his right wrist all the old blood received on their thirteenth birthday to show their family affiliations. In two years, when he turned eighteen, it would have been altered to show his affiliation to his betrothed's family. He heard Amelia's quick intake of breath as she gazed at the marque.

'You walk a dangerous path Seamus of the Hand.'

Seamus froze. How had she known? She could not only read first blood marques, she also knew who he was!

'I don't know what you are talking about. I am Sean,' Seamus blustered.

Ali was looking at Amelia and Seamus, and then back again, clearly confused.

'Seamus, I know who you are, and your family history. I know as you do there are very few families of the old blood with the kind of magic you possess. Your family became entwined with magic—among other things—some generations back when your great-great-grandfather was married to the king of Nataria's granddaughter as part of a peace accord.

'Unknown to the old blood, the king's daughter was a witch. It was the final insult from the king to his new subjects. Ever since then, one child each generation has borne the stigmatism of magic. If it was a girl child, they had a choice. They could leave and live life quietly out of the family and bare no children, or be quietened. If a boy, they would have the magic removed by the rather brutal practice of quietening, or they would be put to death. In this way they had hoped to cleanse the family of the taint of magic blood. But still in each generation one child with magic has been born.

'And you are right that the wizards would more than welcome one of the old blood wishing to develop their magic skills, as they would be the first of their kind at the school. They have been waiting years for such a child to show at their doors. But this would be quite a blow to your family. Can you do that to your father? If you cannot bear to be without magic why not just leave and live a quiet life somewhere?'

All Seamus heard from Amelia was that the wizards would likely take him and his plan would not be thwarted. 'I will do as I planned,' he asserted, not thinking twice about how Amelia had known so much of old blood history. He settled back down thinking his time for questioning was over.

A frowning Amelia sighed. 'I wish you would reconsider, but I can see your mind is made up. If you insist on this journey then it is my duty to help you as best I can. I would suggest you come home with me tomorrow and we make sure you are kitted out for the long road you must travel.'

Seamus, used to having people organise things for him as the son of a duke, did not think to question why Amelia felt she had a duty to help him. However he thanked her for her offer and agreed to head home with her tomorrow. If he were better prepared for travelling he might actually have a chance of getting to the Wizard Isles. His ordeal over, he was pleased attention would now be focused on Ali. What would Amelia make of him?

Aliah squirmed uncomfortably as attention moved to her. Amelia's face was kind but her deep brown eyes were strangely knowing. Would Aliah's story hold up under her scrutiny? She hoped so, as telling the truth might put all of them in danger and she did not want to endanger anyone who tried to help her.

'So, young man, you are heading back home? Which way is that?' Amelia asked.

An easy question, but Aliah could not afford to let down her guard. 'My family have a place not far from Bannock Town.' Well, it was close to the truth, 'So I will be heading north as well.'

'Mmm,' Amelia pondered, rubbing the side of her face as she thought. 'I suppose you have considered the fact that your parents let you go with the sailors, for the money they gained or for other reasons. They may not be as welcoming as you might be expecting when you return home.'

Aliah had not actually considered that. She had felt so sure the right thing to do was find her father and let him know she was all right, and had totally wiped from her mind the circumstances that led to her being on the ship in the first place.

Without knowing what had led to her adventure, Amelia had hit the nail right on the head. If she went home her father would be in serious trouble. Her best bet was to stay away from him and stay anonymous until she knew what had gone on in her absence. However, that did not prevent her from heading towards home, finding out what was going on, and making sure her family were all right.

'I understand what you are saying, and you might well be right.' Aliah looked bleakly at Amelia. 'But I need to at least try to get home and make sure everything is as it should be there. So I will be heading north tomorrow.'

Amelia stared at her for what seemed like an age before turning her attention to pouring the tea and passing round the mugs. Aliah wondered if Amelia always travelled with three bowls and cups, or if she had maybe had a strange feeling that she might need them on this journey.

With Amelia still staring at her, Aliah felt the need to tell her a little more of why her journey was so important.

'It is not just seeing my family that I need to return home for. While I was on board the ship I heard some things that were very worrying. The ship was sailing for Carsten, they had some important cargo for their king. The cargo was going to help the king stir up a war against Aria. I have to go north and warn our king.' Aliah stared Amelia directly in the eye, willing her to understand how important it was that she return home.

Amelia's eyes crinkled at the corners. 'And you will be able to talk to the king about this?'

'My family have served in Bannock Castle for generations. I feel I might have a chance of being listened to. Regardless, I have to try.'

'How very noble of you.' Amelia paused and continued

BEGINNINGS

to look at Aliah, then shook her head. 'I am not sure we have the full truth of you yet, young Ali, but I sense that you are at the centre of something not of your making and you will need all the help you can get before this thing is done. You had best come along with us tomorrow and we will see what we can do to kit you out as well. You will need more than that sword you are carrying to make your way that far north.'

A strange sense of dread fell over Aliah, almost as if she was picking up some of what the woman could sense. She also noticed that Sean's—no, Seamus'—interest had heightened at the mention of a sword and he looked at her a little differently, maybe with a little less superiority. Almost as if he were thinking a boy with a sword may not be quite his social equal, but he might not be far off it.

If only he knew. She smiled to herself, but then shook it off. *He can't know. No one can. It would be too dangerous.*

'Now you two clean up the plates and we'll get some sleep. I want to be off early tomorrow.' Amelia passed her cup to Aliah, and began unrolling her travel swag.

Although Aliah was warm enough with the blanket that had been around her sword she spent a restless night. It was not only that she was not used to sleeping on the ground, she also could not help thinking about her family. Had she caused them any harm by escaping her shipboard captors? How soon would they know she had escaped? It seemed as though she had just fallen asleep when Seamus was waking her with a cup of tea and some bread to break her fast. She was still half asleep when Amelia had them pack up camp and start on their journey to her home on the edge of the Tangled Wood.

3
THE TANGLED WOODS

Aliah's feet hurt. Her arms hurt. Her back hurt. It was not even noon and her body was giving up. If this was how the short walk to the Tangled Woods affected her, how would she ever make it over the mountains? Let alone all the way back to Bannock? Spending a six-days on the boat had definitely left her out of condition.

Amelia had stopped them briefly for a water break and snack of some kind of oat and seed cakes not that long ago, saying that should keep them going until they reached her house. Once there, she would prepare a main meal for them all. Aliah's body had protested when they started out again and had been complaining ever since. As they walked through the wood she caught occasional glimpses of the rolling hills on the other side, but they never seemed to get any closer. Neither Amelia nor Seamus were inclined to talk as they walked, which left Aliah alone with her own thoughts.

She spent most of the morning trying to remember what she could about the Isle of Hand where Seamus must come from. If she remembered her history lessons correctly the island was mostly inhabited by what were now called the old blood, who had fled there as a result of the Natari Invasion. Their King had finally asked what the price for peace was and the Natari King leading the invasion had agreed terms with him.

It was at that time the Southern Duchy was created, which included The Isle of Hand and Port Marden. As a show of good faith, the Natari Emperor had married his granddaughter to the King—now Duke—of Hand's eldest son. Since that time, the Duke of Hand and his people had reluctantly paid homage to whoever ruled Aria.

As time progressed the new nation of Aria had pulled away from the constraints of the Natari Emperor, and the Archduke had become King in his own right. The king was supported by the five dukes, who were meant to be his closest advisors. In reality only four of the five dukes attended Court, or sent their representatives. The Southern Duchy of Hand had preferred to keep to itself.

She also remembered vaguely the old blood were formed into family units and affiliations and that the family of the Hand was the ruling clan. From the conversation last night, Aliah assumed Seamus was a son of the Duke of Hand, who was still known as King by his own people. Aliah tried to assess whether or not that made a difference to how she viewed Seamus. If she were honest, it did not really change anything. She was grateful he had saved her at the markets, and sad that he had to leave his family, but she had known him such a short time it did not really matter who he was. Although it did explain his arrogance, and the name Seamus suited him a little better than Sean had.

After their short break she had tried to fathom out Amelia, which was a little harder. Although she tried to act like a traditional farmer's wife, there was something about her that was a little different. She seemed to "know" or "feel" a lot about them, and it was odd she had come prepared on her journey to meet visitors with extra plates and mugs in her pack. Aliah was sure she also knew rather more about Seamus than she was letting on.

Bored with walking and her own thoughts Aliah decided maybe it was time to find out a little more about the person who seemed so keen to help them. Tucking a stray hair behind her ear, she shuffled up so she could walk beside Amelia, careful not to leave the track as it was now closely bordered by trees and under growth, and she did not want to twist an ankle.

'Ah. Amelia,' she started. 'I was wondering how you knew to bring three sets of eating utensils with you to market?'

Amelia raised an eyebrow. 'Were you just? You are the observant one, aren't you? Perhaps I just had an inkling

Vivienne Lee Fraser

I may have a need of them if I went to this market.'

'Do you not go to every market?' Aliah fished for more information.

'No, I do not. I only go if I have a need for something, or if I feel I need to go there.'

'So, this market trip was for a feeling?' Aliah prompted.

Amelia laughed. 'You are a sharp one, aren't you! Yes, I had a feeling. I often get them when someone needs to see me. Mostly they know to find me in the market as it is a long way to come out to the Tangled Woods. But this time there was no one there, so I am thinking maybe the feeling was for meeting the two of you. There you go, young one, that is enough for you to be getting on with? We are here and we need to get sorted for the evening.'

Without Aliah noticing they had arrived at a paved path leading to a cottage set behind a late-flowering herb garden. The cottage was thatched roofed, as she expected, but it was much larger than she had imagined the cottage of a market gardener to be. It was two storied, and had what looked like a stable behind although she could see no horse, and a paddock beside with a couple of sheep and a cow. On the far side there was a large garden patch, with fruit trees in behind, which ran nearly to the edge of the woods. In between the garden and the house was a water well and a chopping block. It was not the average cottage of a woman who was subsisting on what she grew and sold at market.

'Quit gawking! We have plenty to do before we eat our meal. There is a barn behind the house—beside the stable there—you can put both the baskets in it. I need to go and find Molly.' Amelia put her basket down and headed behind the stables towards the woods, alternating between whistling and calling out, 'Molly!'

Seamus and Aliah looked at each other, then Seamus took the handle from her. 'You take that one.' He pointed to Amelia's basket then took off with the one they had been carrying, her sword still perched on the top. Frowning, she picked up the other basket and followed. By the time she had reached the shed, Seamus had stowed his basket and had her sword out of its sheath, trying a few moves with it.

'Excuse me,' Aliah said in her iciest voice. 'Here I was thinking you were the son of a duke, not a common thief. I will have my sword back.'

'This is no mere sword. It is a work of art and belongs to nobility.' Seamus held the sword up showing its gleaming metal with scrollwork up the shaft and the jewel in the handle. On the blade were the runes her father's blacksmith had carved into it to make the blade strong. 'No common boy sold to work on a ship could have come by a sword like this honestly.' He hefted the sword and tried a couple of moves, getting the balance of it.

Furious, Aliah looked around. There was an old broom handle beside her. She grabbed it, felt its weight, and adjusted her stance. Then with three swipes of the broom, Seamus was on the floor rubbing his arm, the sword no longer in his grasp. Aliah picked up her sword and put it back in its leather scabbard. She placed the broom where she had found it.

'Some people have swords because they deserve them, others because they are given them.' Head held high she stalked out of the shed.

Seamus stood, dusting himself off. How had Ali done that? So he wasn't the best swordsman this side of the dividing mountains but he could handle himself if he had to. Ali had moved so fast he had been off his feet before he even knew he was going to be hit. He finished stowing his basket and left the shed nearly stumbling into a large black horse that was standing by the door. 'Not my day,' he muttered.

Amelia emerged from behind the barn. 'Oh good, you've found Molly. Can you take her to the stable and give her some fresh hay and a feed of grain?'

'You have a horse?' Seamus asked, quizzically. 'Why did you not ride her to market?'

'I just had a feeling that this time she would not be needed. Now off you go. I have to go and get started on the meal.' Amelia headed towards the house where she seemed intent on rounding up Ali, who was practising his sword work in the clear area in front of the house. Seamus paused long enough to see that Ali was putting away the sword in preparation for some task Amelia had given him.

Having stabled Molly, Seamus headed to the well. He drew a bucket of water and washed his face and hands as best he could before entering the cottage. The door opened into a single kitchen and living area. It was dominated by a large wooden table. On the left he could see two doors leading to other rooms, and some stairs that led to a loft room above. At the table Amelia took

BEGINNINGS

some bread dough out of a bowl and began kneading it. Ali followed him in with an armful of wood, which he deposited in the basket beside the open fire. He used one of the smaller logs to stir the banked fire before placing it, and a couple of others, on the now bright embers.

'Thank you, Ali, that will be perfect. The bread dough is nearly ready. Would you mind getting some vegetables from the baskets you put in the barn? We will need them for the stew. And you, Seamus, could get me the dried deer meat from the store room, over there on the left.' Amelia pointed vaguely then carried on, absorbed in her task.

Ali brushed passed Seamus without saying a word, and Seamus headed for the storeroom. He was surprised the room was nearly as large as the cook's pantry in his father's house, and nearly as well stocked. Whoever this woman was, she was not a peasant farmer. He found the dried deer meet hanging from a hook, and shut the door behind him before taking it over to the table. A few minutes later Ali came in with a basket of vegetables and took them over to a large bowl on the bench under the window. He poured water out of a jug and began cleaning off the dirt.

He may have the sword of a noble, but he cleans vegetables like a peasant boy. Seamus slumped down on the bench seat by the table.

'You are not finished yet, young man,' Amelia scolded. 'There are no free rides in this house. You can get yourself up those stairs. In the trunk under the window there should be bedding enough for you to make up two of the beds. Well, off you go then.'

Amelia did not notice Ali's look of dismay as she

mentioned them sharing a room. *Well, if he is going to hold a grudge.* Seamus stomped up the stairs. *Two can play at that game!*

Aliah's heart almost stopped when Amelia asked Seamus to make up two beds in the same room. How could she hide the fact she was a girl when they were sleeping in close quarters? Her hair alone would give it away. Even now she still had her cap on and collar up so no one could see her plait.

'It seems to me you have two choices, Ali.' Amelia's voice startled her. 'We can go into my room and cut your hair short before Seamus comes down and he will be none the wiser. Or you can let him know you are a girl. It won't make much difference to him, either way. But you must do what you feel comfortable with.'

'How …? How did you know?' The surprise nearly caused her to slice her hand instead of the carrot she was holding, meaning she had to keep her eyes on the vegetables in front of her rather than turning around to face Amelia.

'Anyone with eyes can see your shirt is much too bulky for your size. Either you have a deformity, or that is long hair you have tucked in the back.'

'Oh.' Aliah was crestfallen. It would be much more difficult traveling if people knew she was female. People would think it was odd a girl being away from home without a family member. No parent would let their girl child wander the land unattended, no matter how poor they were.

BEGINNINGS

'It does not matter to me whether you be a boy or girl, but if you wish to keep your hair you might as well be yourself here. We can devise something better to manage hiding who you are while you travel.' Aliah looked up saw Amelia was smiling encouragingly at her.

Somewhat relieved, Aliah took off her cap and jacket, and pulled her long blonde braid out from inside the shirt. It was somewhat of a relief not to have it tucked in there.

'Now we have that sorted, can you please cut the vegetables and meat and put them into that pot so we can begin making a stew for supper.'

Seamus was not the best at bed making as he was used to having servants do it for him. As his circumstances were somewhat altered he really should give this bed-making a good go, especially as this may not be the last time he had to do it. He doubted trainee wizards had servants.

He found sheets and blankets in the chest under the window as Amelia had said. There were three beds in the room, arranged against the walls. He made up the one closest to the chimney and put his jacket on it. At least he would be warm tonight. He then made up the bed furthest away by the opening of the stairs for Ali. If he wanted to be standoffish, Seamus would certainly help him. Job done, he climbed back down stairs.

Amelia was putting two bread tins in an alcove by the fire, and at the table Ali was chopping meat and putting it in a pot. Ali reached to take some vegetables off the workbench and Seamus' eyes widened in astonishment. Ali had a long plait of hair down his back.

It took a moment, then it hit him. Ali was a GIRL. Not only had she fooled him for nearly two days, SHE had knocked him off his feet as if he were no bigger than his younger brother. He was just about to say something when Amelia caught his eye. She shook her head and looked at Ali. The message was clear. Now was not the time to talk about this.

'If you have finished the beds you can go out and start work on the woodpile. You will find an axe inside the barn. We will call you when dinner is ready.' Amelia covered the pot for the stew and put it on the rack over the fire.

The sun was just about setting when Amelia finally called him in to dinner. He had managed to double the size of the woodpile before cleaning the axe and putting it back. He had to admit there was something satisfying in chopping wood. Maybe it was the manual labour, or maybe it was because he could put his worries to the back of his mind and do something that would actually benefit himself and others. Whatever it was, he was ready for a big meal.

He cleaned up in the small room off the pantry and sat down at the table just as Amelia placed three bowls of a thick meaty stew down beside three sets of cutlery. To accompany the meal was a fresh loaf of bread, rich creamy butter, and a white cheese. Amelia took the place at the head of the table and Ali sat down opposite him, still avoiding his eyes. Once they were seated, Amelia said a blessing to the goddess for their bounty and they all began to eat.

BEGINNINGS

As Seamus stopped to butter some bread, Amelia put down her fork and looked at the two young people.

'Well we can all see now that Ali—'

'Aliah,' Ali interrupted.

'Aliah, is a girl. That is enough on that matter unless Aliah wants to add anything?'

Aliah shook her head.

'All right, then. I know we are all tired, but we need to make some plans. Summer has drawn to a close, and it looks like we will not have much of a fall before the snows this year, so you two cannot be dilly dallying for too long if you wish to head to Bannock before those on your tails catch you up. Agreed?'

Seamus lifted his head and nodded. He noticed Aliah continued to eat and said nothing. Amelia obviously took her silence as agreement as she continued to speak.

'Right then. Next step, as you are both heading the same way I propose that you travel together.' Anticipating both their objections she held up her hand and continued before they could interrupt her.

'Hear me out here. It is for both your benefits I am proposing this. Seamus, your family is looking for a boy traveling by himself, not a young man escorting his sister. And Aliah, you would only be able to keep up your appearance as a boy for so long, and you cannot travel by yourself as a girl. If you travel as siblings and have a purpose—taking Aliah to meet her intended husband—then you have a disguise that suits you both and puts your pursuers off your scent.'

Seamus looked up at Amelia in surprise, then turned to Aliah. She seemed to be seriously considering Amelia's words. Maybe it was a sensible thing to do? Aliah voiced her agreement and he reluctantly also agreed.

'Now that is settled, I propose we spend a six-day getting together the things you will need for your journey, and on the new first-day you shall set out. That does not give us much time to dry food and make the things you need, but any longer and you may not make it through the Ariel Mountains before the first snow.'

Again Seamus and Aliah looked at each other, both frowning a little. 'A whole six-day?' Seamus asked, facing Amelia and voicing both their concerns.

'It is a long journey you are undertaking, children, and most of it will be in the cold of fall, and maybe even in an early winter. You'll be needing warm clothing and plenty of dried food. And that will have to be gathered and made as I do not have that sort of stock here, nor do I have enough coin to provide for both of you. What we can do is make the most of the bounty here and that will take time.'

'I have a little money,' Seamus admitted, taking his coin purse from his pocket.

'And I also have a little. And we can work for food and coin on our journey.' Aliah broke in.

'That coin would not be nearly enough to see you to Bannock, Seamus. And, Aliah, yes you could work,' Amelia confirmed. 'But while that would save you time now it would add time onto your journey and you would definitely be traveling through winter. And you need to consider how it will look, a young girl heading off to a wedding not fully provisioned by her family. Your cover would be full of holes, ones that those following you would definitely see through.'

Seamus listened as Amelia spoke, respecting good planning when he heard it. He told her he thought it would work. He had been on many a hunting party and knew that preparation was essential for a good outcome. Aliah knew the battle was lost and concentrated on finishing her meal.

With the big decisions all made, they finished their dinner and cleaned up in silence. Amelia put the kettle on to make a soothing tea, which both Aliah and Seamus declined, their weary bodies needing a good night's sleep.

As they climbed the stairs Seamus cringed with embarrassment at Aliah's dismay when she discovered the bed he had made for her. Wishing to make amends he remembered there had been more blankets in the chest, and some old sheets cut into lengths of rag for cleaning. He made rope from some of the rags, and strung it up in the rafters between the beds and hung a blanket over top.

'It might make you feel more comfortable,' he smiled sheepishly at Aliah, and to his surprise she beamed a smile back.

'Thank you,' she said. 'That's the nicest thing anyone has done for me in a while.' Seamus ducked his head so she would not see the blush rising from below his collar.

The bed was warm and comfortable, especially after sleeping on the ground the night before. It was not long before Aliah's rhythmic breathing filled the room, and soon Seamus was sleeping the deep sleep of the exhausted.

4
DAWN TIL DUSK

For the next two days Amelia worked her two young
guests from dawn til dusk, and beyond. Realising
Seamus was more proficient with the bow than a sword,
Amelia sent him into the woods to hunt small animals.
Aliah and Amelia then prepared the animals to dry in
the smokehouse at the back of the barn. By the end of
the second day the smokehouse was full of meat.

The following day Amelia started them on picking the
last of the fruit from her trees and the last of the berries

from the bushes in the woods. They also pulled the last of the herbs and vegetables from her garden. These were laid out on drying racks in the barn ready to pack. Day four was left for going through Amelia's own winter stores to see what she could spare for their journey. They packaged up flour, grains and pulses, and two thick yellow cheeses to add to their travel packs.

Amelia showed them how to cook their dried stores into a tasty meal in one of the billy pots she had included with their utensils. She also made up for them a small store of dried leaves for various tisanes to help with common ailments, and a larger portion of tea leaves for a restorative evening drink. There were also some herbs for flavouring their meals. With the food mostly sorted, the morning of day five, Amelia took them out to the barn. Standing at the bottom of the loft stairs she pointed upwards.

'Up there you will find trunks filled with all the things I have needed over the years. If I remember there should be a large traveling pack and a slightly smaller one that I have used for various journeys. Both have seen better days, but they should do this one last trip.'

'There should also be a bedroll or two, old water skins, and wet weather gear. Have a look through and see what is still usable. Also, Seamus, you may find a set of throwing knives in one of the trunks. If you are anything like the rest of your family, knives and bows will be your weapons of choice. I have chores to do, let me know if you need anything.' With that she departed, leaving them to their own devices.

It was dirty, dusty work but by the time they had gone through the first two trunks they had found travel packs and bedrolls. They took these downstairs and beat the dust from them, then hung them to air over a line they strung between the stable and the barn. They also found four water skins that would likely see them through the journey.

The third trunk was the largest, and they had left it until last. It proved to be the most interesting. On the top was the set of knives Amelia had mentioned to Seamus, and these he put over by the water skins to be cleaned and oiled. The rest of the trunk was full of clothing of various descriptions for both sexes. They took it all out to go through and were just closing the lid when voices drifted in from outside. They could not see anything out of the barn loft window, so they crept downstairs and went round the back of the house to sneak a peak at what was going on.

In front of the house, Amelia had been busy tidying up in the garden preparing it for a winter crop, but had been interrupted by a young squire. He had the same dark eyes and hair as Seamus, although it was cut and tamed into a bob, and he was gesturing wildly as they talked.

'They are saying he used magic to escape, Amelia.' The boy's voice drifted to them.

Amelia patted his arm in an effort to calm him down. 'You know people like to make up stories to make things seem more exciting.' Amelia then took his arm and walked him to the path that led back to Port Marden. To Seamus' surprise, the young squire bent and hugged Amelia before getting back on his horse and heading off.

He must have gasped out loud as Aliah turned to him, a look of surprise on her rather dirty face. 'What?' she asked.

'That is my father's head squire, my cousin, Liam. What was he doing here? And why was Amelia hugging him?' He frowned and bit his bottom lip.

'We won't find out squatting here.' Aliah stood and walked around to where Amelia watched the squire head back to Port Marden. When he was out of sight she motioned for Seamus to join them. Amelia reluctantly tore her gaze from the departing rider and wiped her hands on her apron. She looked at her two guests as if she were about to say something, then shook her head.

'I guess we can break for the midday meal early, we need to talk. Aliah if you can get the food ready, Seamus and I will tidy up.' And without another word she headed back to the garden.

Seamus and Aliah exchanged a quizzical look and, shrugging their shoulders, went to do as Amelia had asked. When they were seated at the table Amelia waited until after the blessing before she began her explanation.

'I take it you saw young Liam, Seamus?' Seamus nodded as he continued eating, not wanting to show how much his stomach had been churning since he had seen his childhood friend. 'Well, for some time he has shared a confidence with your father that perhaps it is time you knew of as well.'

At this Seamus did look up from his meal. Amelia was staring into her bowl and would not meet his eyes.

'When I was a little younger than you are now I started experiencing dreams. They were different to normal dreams in that a day or two after I had them they seemed to come true. I was frightened. I believed because I dreamt things I was the actual cause. I would dream that someone would fall over and break something, and then that would happen. It was like I was ill-wishing them. I started to not want to sleep.

'My mother noticed a change in me and after weeks of her coaxing I finally blurted out my secret. Far from being shocked and appalled, my mother took me in her arms and started crying. She explained to me I was not causing things to happen, I was merely seeing the future, and it was something others of my family had experienced. It made me feel a little better until she told me I must never tell another living soul what I could do. After she extracted my promise we never spoke of what she called my gift again.

'Just before my sixteenth birthday, I had a dream. My younger brother was going hunting and he was to have the honour of dealing the killing blow to the wild boar for the first time. I dreamt the boar would severely wound him and he would not be able to walk again. He was but a year younger than I and we were very close. I could not stand by and let that happen to him. So I crept into his room the night before the hunt and begged him not to go. He thought I was being a silly girl worrying needlessly about him. So I told him about my dreams, thinking it was the only way he would listen to me and stay safe. I thought he would understand and keep my secret.

'Rather than thank me he went straight to our father. I had not counted on my family's abhorrence of what they call mage-craft being stronger than his love for me. My father locked me in my room for being "hysterical", and the hunt went ahead as planned. My brother never dealt that first killing blow. The boar attacked him as I had predicted it would, and it was only because of his foreknowledge that my father was prepared and he was able to kill the boar before it did any lasting damage.

'Ironically, I had managed to save my brother, but the boar charging as in my dream sealed my fate. My father imposed the Rule of the Hand and told me that on my 18th birthday I could choose. I could leave the Isle of Hand, or I could take the honourable option of being quietened. I chose to leave the Isle and all my family. On my 18th birthday I was given my dowry and sent into the world to find my way on my own.

'I had planned to travel as far away as I possibly could from here, but the night before I was to leave my brother came to my room and begged for me not to go far. He felt guilty for the outcome of his actions, although he believed they were right and proper, but he said he could not bear for me to be completely estranged. He found this farm and agreed a price with the farmer that was only a small portion of my dowry. If I moved here we could visit and stay in contact, and maybe one day the Rule of Hand would change and I could come home.' Amelia stopped to take a drink.

Seamus stared incredulously at Amelia. He had realised she was telling a different version of a story he had grown up hearing. The story of how his father had been gashed by a boar during his first lead of the hunt. Seamus looked more closely at the woman sitting in front of him, noting especially the dark black eyes she shared with his father. And although her hair was a little lighter than his father's she definitely resembled him, perhaps more than Seamus did himself. But most of all, it was

BEGINNINGS

the wry smile she gave as she told her story that reminded him of the King of Hand.

'You are my father's sister. The one they call Amalie. We were told you died.'

'Yes, that was my name a long time ago. I will never go by that name again. I am now Amelia. And to all but a few of our family I am dead. And I am living proof that although your father upholds the Rule of Hand when it comes to those born with mage powers, he has a strong sense of family. He has never been able to completely let me go. He visits sometimes, and has taken Liam into his confidence so that I may have company when he cannot come. He does not know it, but your mother and our younger brother also visit from time to time. They stop by the markets when I attend, sometimes I am forewarned that they need me and I will go especially to the markets to meet with them. It is through all of this contact that I know of you and your family. I know you almost as well as I would have had I lived with you.

'I only tell you this now Seamus because this is your last chance to reconsider your course of action. I told you before that your father would most likely not expect you to take your life, or live without using magic. I believe that because of how he has treated me, it is likely he would allow you to live a quiet life away from the Isle. Liam confirmed this today. He came to ask me to look out for you. Your father believes you have found out about me and you might come here. He sent Liam to ask if I would be prepared to let you live with me and carry on the farm after I am gone from this world to the next. I agreed that would be an option, should you come here.

So, I ask you again Seamus, do you really want to go to the Wizard Isles to train?'

Seamus sat still for a while, his eyes not focusing on anything. In his mind he was going through all his options, but he really could see no other way forward. Soon the silence in the room became too much, even for him.

'So,' he broke the silence. 'The alternatives I face are death, having my magic removed possibly resulting in death, or following in your footsteps?'

'That is correct,' Amelia told him.

'Just so as I understand the full deal here, would I be permitted to marry and have children? Or have I guessed correctly that part of this arrangement would be I never have children so I do not pass on the taint of magic?'

Amelia nodded. 'Again, that is correct.'

'Do you believe that there is any chance I would be allowed to keep my magic and return home?' Seamus looked Amelia straight in the eyes.

Amelia shook her head. 'As the Rule of Hand now stands, that would never be an option.'

'If I don't have the protection of the School of Wizards then all my other options are about having a half-life, never being able to fully be who I am. No disrespect to you Amelia, but I cannot live that way.'

Tears came to Seamus' eyes as the full impact of the last few days hit him. Now that his family knew he had magic, there was no way they would let him learn how to control it and return home. There was only one future for him that allowed him to be himself.

Amelia frowned, 'As a woman my choices were even

fewer than yours as there is no school for women with magical abilities. But knowing what I know now having lived my life, I wished I had half your courage when I made my choice.' Amelia took a deep breath. 'Right then, back to work. Liam is a smart boy and he will have seen the stripping of my gardens and the travel packs out the back. He may not have fully understood what they meant yet, but it will not be long before it dawns on him and he will be back. We had best plan for your journey to begin tomorrow.'

Seamus looked at Aliah and she returned his gaze, frowning a little. 'Are you sure this is what you really want to do?' she asked him.

He forced a smile. 'Not really, no. But at least it is a plan, and it is my plan.'

She smiled back and tucked a stray bit of hair behind her ear. 'Right, well we should get started then.'

For the rest of the afternoon Aliah and Seamus went through the clothing in the third trunk to ensure they had a set of clothes to travel in, a change of clothes, changes of under garments, a woollen cloak, and oilskins to keep off the rain. They hung them out in the barn to air overnight.

They then began wrapping the food for travel and putting them in the packs. Seamus sharpened his knives, made some arrows, restocked Amelia's woodpile for the winter and re-dug her garden making it ready for replanting in the spring.

After they ate a late dinner they packed their changes of clothes ready to leave early the next morning. While they were in the process of redistributing the food to even the weight, Amelia appeared from her bedroom with a sword belt and gave it, not to Aliah, but to Seamus.

'You will need this to carry Aliah's sword,' she said.

'I can carry my own sword,' Aliah protested, frowning.

'I know you can dear,' Amelia said wearily. 'But most girls going to meet her husband would not be gallivanting round the countryside with a sword at her side, would she? If she could defend herself, why would she need her brother to escort her?'

'But I am useless with a sword,' Seamus grumbled. 'As Aliah has already demonstrated. And if I carry this, how will I be able to get at a weapon I can use like my bow or knives?'

'If I am to do all your thinking for you, how will you get on when you leave here tomorrow?' Amelia smiled at them to take the sting out of her words. 'Firstly, Seamus, a bow will be of little use to you so that will be staying behind. Secondly, if you wear the sword on your left hand side, then your right hand is free to throw knives. If Aliah walks on your left she will be able to access the sword easily. Aliah, you may want to practice drawing your sword while you are walking *before* you get into any trouble.'

'Ah.' Seamus grinned. 'And if we do get into trouble it will create an element of surprise. They won't expect knives from my right hand, nor will they expect a sword-wielding woman. I like it.' His grin widened, then disappeared as he realised they would be leaving Amelia and the safety of her home tomorrow. He did not know how he could ever repay her kindness, and he regretted he had not had time to get to know his newfound Aunt better.

BEGINNINGS

Aliah shrugged as if not carrying her own sword did not matter. But it did. It frustrated her when people thought girls could not look after themselves. She also knew Amelia was right though, it was the best way to travel. For now.

Finishing her packing and doing up her pack she realised she was a little concerned about how they would fare without their host's help along the way. Especially her ability to smooth things over between her and Seamus when they could not agree. They would truly be on their own and would have to learn to give and take. She promised herself that once she was home she would find a way to repay Amelia for her generosity and all she had done to help them on their journey.

5
THE JOURNEY BEGINS

Seamus' body was still in sleep mode when Amelia woke them. In fact, it was sure it had just laid down. Sleepily pulling himself out of bed he left Aliah to get dressed into her traveling clothes while he dressed before the fire downstairs. The tunic and hose he wore were of good quality, but the brown and cream woollen fabric was a bit more rustic than he was used to. Amelia had said his father stayed at the cottage sometimes and these were the clothes he wore when he was there. He pulled on his own boots and went out to the woodpile to get a days supply of wood in.

Amelia had started to prepare the porridge for breakfast when he brought the wood in. She was half-listening to Aliah with a decidedly unsympathetic ear. Instead of the tunic and hose Aliah had laid out last night, she was wearing a dress and tunic in similar fabrics and colours to his own. She had a cloak thrown over her shoulders, and bare feet.

'But it will be so uncomfortable to walk in, and I will not be able to wield my sword so easily.' She demonstrated for Amelia. 'Can I not have back my tunic and leggings? I can change back into these when we are in sight of any towns.'

'Your attire is entirely appropriate for a girl from a respectable family traveling to meet her husband. Boy's clothing is not. Trust me on this. You will get used to travelling in a dress, even though it seems cumbersome at the moment.' Amelia put the pot over the fire for the porridge to cook as Aliah looked daggers at her back.

'Now you have a change of clothes in your bag, and I have also put in a pair of indoor shoes. While you are travelling it is best to wear your boots. That will not be too uncommon a sight. However if you must stay at an inn you will need to change your footwear to something considered more suitable.'

Aliah stomped to the bench, flicked her skirts out of the way and sat to tie her boots, all the while throwing rebellious looks towards Amelia. Amelia, oblivious to the death stares, went into her bedroom and came back out with a money pouch.

BEGINNINGS

'Seamus, you had best have this. It is not much, but it will be enough for you to sleep a few nights at an inn if needs be, and to replenish your supplies if you are careful.' This earned her another angry stare from Aliah, but surely she knew people would expect the male in the party to be carrying money.

Seamus was reluctant to take the purse for other reasons. 'You might need that money, Amelia, I cannot take it. Besides, I have a little money of my own.'

'Oh, my boy, my family have not abandoned me completely. I have only to ask and this money will be replaced. I will wait a while though, as I do not want them to become suspicious of my wanting coin so close to your visit.' She tucked the purse inside his tunic, and began serving the porridge. Seamus made a note to split the money with Aliah later just in case something happened to him.

It was a quiet meal. None of those sitting around the table wanted to think about the fact this would be the last time they would eat together. Lost in his thoughts, Seamus nearly knocked over his bowl when Amelia suddenly jumped to her feet.

'Someone is coming,' she said. 'We have but a few minutes. Your father, I think. And young Liam. And some of his men. If you are set on this course of action rather than fixing things with your father, you need to gather your belongings and go wait behind the barn. When they come inside, take to the woods alongside the track, not *on* the track. I will delay your father for as long as I can to give you a head start. Once your father and his men pass on the way back to Port Marden, you will be safe to come out of the woods.'

Amelia quickly gathered their plates and hid them under some logs in the wood basket. He and Aliah closed their travel packs and pulled the straps over their shoulders, then put on their capes so their packs were covered. They said only quick farewells as Amelia hurriedly bundled them outside.

'Goddess speed, my young friends,' she said as she shut the door behind them.

Seamus and Aliah hurried to crouch behind the barn before the company arrived. They had just settled when horses and riders burst into the clearing in front of the cottage. From their hiding place they could see four men on horseback wearing travelling clothes with their hoods pulled up, and swords strapped to their hips. They entered the clearing in front of the house and leapt from their saddles. Three of them handed their reins to the fourth and headed for the cottage. There was a knock at the door, some muted voices, and the sound of a door closing.

'What do we do now?' Aliah whispered. 'That man out front will surely see us if we head for the woods.'

'Just wait a minute,' Seamus whispered back. 'He will need to water the horses and when he heads to the well we will take our chance.'

Aliah voiced her agreement.

No sooner had Seamus finished speaking than the man tethered the horses to a tree branch, and headed over to the well. Seamus grabbed Aliah's hand and they made a break for the trees, running as fast and quietly as they could, packs bouncing uncomfortably on their backs. They managed to duck in behind the horses and

BEGINNINGS

hide in the brush, just as the man came back with his bucket of water.

As they crouched in the damp brush Seamus cursed himself as they now could not move to the track without disturbing the horses. He looked at Aliah, signalling for her to stay still. She nodded her understanding. Chewing his lip, he considered their options. Before he could think of any, Aliah half stood and threw something back towards the barn. The horses tugged at their reigns and the soldier stood to attention, looking where the noise had come from. Aliah grabbed his hand and jerked him towards the track.

When they reached the tree cover, they stopped and looked back. The soldier had just disappeared behind the barn.

'What did you think you were doing?' Seamus hissed angrily at Aliah.

'Getting us out of a tight situation.' She smiled infuriatingly back at him.

'We might have been seen.' He growled at her.

'But we weren't.' She answered through gritted teeth. 'Come on, if we don't move now they will definitely see us.' She stalked off through the trees. He reluctantly followed.

'That was just plain risky.' He muttered to himself as he walked. 'We so might have been seen.'

'You know I can hear you?' she whispered. 'At least we are on our way, not still waiting for you to have an idea.' She flicked her plait behind her and carried on walking.

What annoyed him most was she was right. He had

had no idea how to get past the horses.

They walked in silence until they could no longer hear the horses snuffling behind them. The path they took was not an easy one. There was a lot of undergrowth grabbing at their ankles, and a couple of times they lost the track and had to double back, least they get even more lost.

'Phew!' Seamus said as he checked they could still see the track from where they were. 'This is not a great way to start.' That was as close as he was going to get to thanking her for getting them away.

'It was close,' Aliah agreed, ready to forget his earlier anger. 'And I did not even get time to properly thank Amelia for all she has done.' She finished, sadly.

'I think she knows how much you appreciated it,' Seamus consoled her; it was the least he could do given his earlier behaviour. 'She has a knack for knowing a lot of things. What she would really want is for us to be careful so all her hard work does not get wasted. Come on! We need to keep moving as neither of us are safe this side of the Ariel Mountains.'

'Are you quite sure you know where we are going?' Aliah asked as they started towards Port Marden.

Seamus reached into his tunic and pulled out a piece of parchment. 'Amelia helped me draw this map last night and we worked out the best route through the mountains. Beyond that, she has little knowledge, so we will be on our own.' He put the map back inside his tunic. 'I can talk you through it when we stop for the night.'

'Yes, please.'

They walked in silence for a time, keeping their feet from

the grasp of the undergrowth took all their concentration. Tree branches snatched at their packs and they had to make detours round trees and bits of scrub. Every now and then they stopped to ensure they had not gone too far into the woods and they could still see the track.

'Blast it!' Seamus exclaimed as his boot came off his foot for the third time.

'What was that?'

Seamus and Aliah both froze. Neither of them had said that.

Seamus motioned to Aliah. He could see a large fallen tree, and he directed her to it. Following, boot in hand, he slid in underneath beside her. Locked eyes, they both held their breath as footsteps drew closer.

'I was sure I heard something.' A voice was right above them. The tree slipped as it took the weight of someone.

'Careful. I am not carrying you out of here if you break something.' The other voice was to the front of them to the right. Seamus could just make out the colours of the Hand Guard. In fact, if the soldier turned now he would be able to see them both.

Aliah's eyes were wide with worry and he silently pleaded with her not to do anything hasty. The log shifted again as the soldier above them stepped down in front of their hiding place, effectively blocking his comrades' view of them.

'Can you see anything?' he asked.

'No.'

They both paused. Coming from the track was the sound of a horse.

'Come on. Let's go and see what the others have found.'

The man in front of them climbed back up on the log. Seamus held in a groan as the weight of the log pressed on his leg. When the weight released he heard the two men heading back for the track.

He put his finger to his lips, and they waited. They could hear three voices, but could not make out what they were saying. Finally the sound of horses leaving filled the woods, and they both let out a sigh of relief.

They pulled themselves out from under the tree and dusted themselves off. Considering the length of time they had been on the ground they were not too dirty. Just as they were about to move, the sound of more hoof beats stopped them, and they ducked behind a tree in time to see two horses head back towards Port Marden.

'By my count, that makes only three men returning from Amelia's, unless there are other people using this track.'

Seamus agreed. 'It is unlikely farmers out this way would be riding horses, they would most likely be pulling a cart.'

'What do you think happened to the other one?'

'Well,' Seamus said, thoughtfully. 'Either my father left him behind because he was not sure Amelia was telling the truth, or he left him to come slowly after, hoping to find us on the trail, *or* he is helping Amelia with something and will follow later. I really don't know.'

Aliah nodded her understanding. 'So do we risk the track?'

'I think it will be all right. We should hear the other horse coming. So long as we keep our ears open and be ready to duck into the undergrowth if we hear anything, we will be fine out of the woods.'

Aliah nodded again. 'And we should rest only in secluded places off the track,' she added.

Leaving the forest, they carried on their journey in silence, a bit fearful they might miss the sounds of a quieter rider if they talked. However the rest of the days journey was uneventful, if a little slower than their trip to Amelia's had been.

They stopped for the day on the edge of the woods near Port Marden. They found a quiet clearing just off the main track. Even though they still had at least a candle-mark more of light, they did not want to risk the open space the road took to the Ariel mountains, in case they were spotted by the man who had stayed behind.

After they had eaten and tided up, Seamus showed Aliah the map he and Amelia had made. 'She suggested we go the longer route through the High Pass towards Sunnydale.' Seamus showed her. 'It will take a little longer, but it is not the route we will be expected to take so we may be a little safer. We should be able to find a merchant train going through the mountains, and they might let us travel with them if we are lucky.'

'I would rather travel alone,' Aliah said. 'Less questions that way and we cannot be caught out in our lies.'

'But we would have more protection from bandits and we would be better hidden from those following us,' Seamus countered. 'Anyway, we do not need to decide now. What we do need is to get some sleep as I want to leave early tomorrow so we can pass Port Marden before the gates open and someone chances to see us.' With that, he snuggled into his bedroll and pulled his cloak over him to keep off the night chill. Aliah sat frowning into the fire for a moment longer, then followed his lead.

The next morning they packed up camp quickly and filled their water skins. Eating some of the fruity travel bread Amelia and Aliah had made, they started at a brisk pace. As with the day before they spoke little as they walked so they could listen for the sounds of other travellers and leave the road if they needed. Aliah had difficulty keeping up with Seamus' long strides. Her legs were tired and sore from the walk yesterday, and they seemed very sluggish this morning.

After she had stumbled a couple of times she stopped them at the edge of the Tangled Woods. 'Seamus, I know you want to be past Port Marden early but I cannot keep up this pace!'

Seamus looked down at Aliah in surprise, as if he was just noticing for the first time that she was a good deal shorter than him. Aliah was tall for a girl, but Seamus himself was quite tall and she stood only as high as his shoulder. There was no way she could keep up with his long stride for any length of time. He looked ahead. 'We still need to walk quickly for this bit because we will be exposed as we leave the woods and head for the mountains. Once we are a little ways from the gate we can slow down.'

Aliah sighed deeply. 'All right, I will try and keep up.' Taking a deep breath she steeled herself to keep the fast pace, looking forward to the promise of slowing down once they passed the gates. By they time they reached the crossroads, where they had decided to follow Amelia's suggestion and take the high road, Aliah's legs were burning.

'Can we stop for a rest?' Aliah hated to ask, but she really needed a break.

Before Seamus could respond the sound of hoof beats filled the air. She looked around but could not see anywhere they could hide, so Aliah moved to Seamus' left hand side, ready to reach for her sword if she needed to.

'All we can do is walk and hope that they do not come close enough to recognise you,' she said. 'We'll put up our hoods to hide our faces. If they ask, you are Sean and I am your sister, Ali. Maybe the different names might put them off.'

They pulled up their hoods and continued on. The hoof beats got closer, then stopped. Aliah looked behind them to see a rider from the Isle of Hand at the crossroads. She waved and he glanced at her before turning his horse towards the Port, where the gates had already opened.

'Hopefully he will have thought we were early birds through the gate and will not give us another thought.' Aliah ran to catch Seamus up. Seamus merely grunted in return.

Excitement over, they carried on walking. The particular pass they were taking through the Ariel Mountains was not much used, but as the sun rose higher in the sky they heard the sounds of another horse and rider behind them. Fearing the worst, they moved to the side of the road and prepared to fight if need be. It was not long before the rider came into sight, and they sighed with relief as they realised it was only a Duke's Messenger, not someone sent by Seamus' father for them.

Still, the messenger slowed and stopped when he saw them. 'Good day. You are headed over the pass to Sunnydale?'

'Yes,' Seamus answered before she could. 'My sister's betrothed lives not far from there.'

'You might want to re-think your timing. Word is there is a big storm coming in from the sea and it will hit the coast within the next day or so. It will bring with it early snow I am told. I am sent to turn travellers back and advise others to take shelter. You have not yet gone too far so I advise you turn back.'

'Thank you for the warning,' Seamus called as the messenger rode on.

'We must turn back.' Aliah insisted. 'Maybe we can stay with Amelia until the storm passes.' Aliah looked at Seamus, who was frowning and chewing his lip.

'I have hunted in these mountains, and there are plenty of caves. If we push on today and make a good pace tomorrow, we can find a cave before the storm comes and hunker down there until it passes.' Seamus looked at her. 'I worry if we go back now my father will find us at Amelia's, and staying anywhere else is too risky. We also run the risk of being stuck at Amelia's until after winter if the mountains become un-passable. Not to mention the fact you want to let the king know about a potential invasion. That information would be too late if we got stuck for the winter.'

Aliah reviewed the arguments he presented. Although the risk of getting caught was not so great for her, she did not fancy making the journey home alone, and she

BEGINNINGS

did need to get news of the potential invasion to the king. She did not want to wait for winter to pass before she even started out for home. Shrugging her shoulders she carried on walking.

The going that day was quite flat and not too strenuous. Not long before they stopped for their evening meal the terrain started to get a little steeper and they entered the foothills of the Ariel Mountains.

Once again, they broke camp early the next morning as Seamus wanted to push on up into the mountains. They did, however, take the time to strap their left over firewood to their packs in case they could not find any further up. Before starting out, they agreed at noon they would stop and find shelter enough to see them through the storm.

It was a slow, tedious trek up through the foothills. Aliah's muscles were still sore from two days of walking and going up hill was making them even worse. From the strain on Seamus' face it was obvious he was also having difficulty, so she kept her complaints to herself.

After a candle-mark or so they had a brief rest beside a stream to refilled the water bags and have some trail bread. Aliah took the opportunity to search the sky behind them for signs of the storm. The sky looked clear enough, but without being able to see back towards the coast she could not judge how long they had before the storm hit. Seamus, noting her concern, hurried to tie the water bottles to their packs and start moving again.

'We had better get our wet weather gear out, just in case,' he advised. 'We are a long way from where I had hoped we would be by now and we may not reach the caves before the bad weather hits us.'

They found their waterproof capes, put them on and over their packs, and started out again. Aliah was not only tired, but also hot. The capes made it difficult to move and in the near midday heat they were stifling. However, as they trudged ever higher, the temperature began to drop and Aliah was grateful for the extra layer of clothing. Midday came and went without them breaking their journey as they were not high enough yet to find a cave for shelter. They trudged on, chewing some trail bread to ease their hunger as the first drops of rain began to fall.

The heavy rain started, each footstep treacherous as water began to run down the trail. The bottom of Aliah's dress was heavy with water and mud and she cursed Amelia for insisting she wear it.

'We have to keep going,' Seamus encouraged her. 'We are not far from some decent sized caves and we will need solid shelter once the storm fully hits us.'

Aliah grumbled under her breath, but carried on. There was sense in what Seamus said, but that did not mean she had to like it.

As if she were not uncomfortable enough, rain began dripping down inside her cape. By the time they reached the mountains proper they were soaked through, and the wind was starting to pick up speed. Aliah could see no further than Seamus' hunched figure in front of her. Still they kept going, with Seamus repeating, 'Not long now', every few minutes.

Not long now ended up being really too long when Seamus finally led them off the main path, down a narrow track, and into a clearing that miraculously contained a cave mouth sheltered from the storm. Seamus had a grin on his face as if to say, 'See, I told you I would find shelter for us.'

There was little light outside the cave, and even less when they got inside. Seamus reached out and Aliah heard some shuffling, then with a 'snick' the darkness was brightened with light.

'My father's men have used this cave before. Each person replaces the torch before leaving so the next inhabitants have light.' He was still smiling as he pulled Aliah further inside the cave. He used the light from the torch to check they were the only life in there. Once he was satisfied, he put the torch up in a groove in the wall.

A shivering Aliah had already taken off her waterproof cloak and was beginning to open her pack for dry clothes when Seamus interrupted her. 'Fire first for survival.'

It was all she could do to stop herself from rolling her eyes.

'There should be some dry wood in the back. If you get that, I will have a look around for more wood out front to add to what we already have on our packs. It will need to dry out, but we do not know how long the storm will keep us here, and what we do not use we can leave for the next travellers.'

As he left to go back into the storm, Aliah cursed him under her breath even as she shivered her way to the back of the cave to find wood and some tinder. She dumped it into the depression in the floor in the middle of the cave, which had obviously been used for a fire pit in the past. Setting up the tinder, she stacked some of the wood to the side to be used later. Some of the longer sticks she leaned against the cave walls as makeshift drying racks for their clothes. As she waited for Seamus to return she kept warm by pacing out the cave. Ten steps from side to side, thirteen steps from back to front. She was nearly bowled over by Seamus returning with his arms full of wood.

'I have placed some more outside by the door in case we need it,' he grimaced. 'The storm is really coming in, if you need to go outside for umm ... er ... you know.' He blushed. 'I would do it now, the storm is coming in fast.'

Aliah blushed a little herself, realising she did need to go out and do exactly that. In her embarrassment she left without her waterproof and did not realise she would need it until the driving rain hit her. Too proud to go back in, she ducked behind a tree and tried to shelter as she relieved herself. Just as she stood to return to the cave the wind rose and the steady rain became hail and sleet. She fought her way back to the entrance against the elements, arriving even colder and wetter than she had been when she left.

Seamus had a small fire going and looked up at her as she came in, frowning at her bedraggled state. 'Best you get out of those clothes and into something dry fast,' he said as he moved so his back was to her, to allow her some privacy.

Feeling like a reprimanded child, Aliah fumbled out of her now drenched clothing. Her freezing fingers made it difficult to undo the fastenings and she got tangled in her heavy, wet skirt. She pulled on dry underclothes. Not wanting to get her spare clothes dirty she wrapped her sleeping blanket around herself. Satisfied she was respectable, she told Seamus he could turn around. Then, to allow him time to change, she moved from the fire and, still shivering, she hung her clothes over the makeshift rack. By the time she had finished hanging up her skirt and shirt Seamus was beside her hanging his wet clothes.

'I will make us some tea and something to eat while you get warm.' He handed her his blanket and went to their packs to get what he needed. Gratefully Aliah drew the extra blanket around herself, then dragged some of the rounder logs of dried wood over so they could use them as back rests. Having pulled out their bedrolls, she made two comfortable nests on either side of the fire. She curled up inside her blankets, and watched Seamus as he poured hot water into two mugs, then began making a stew from their stores.

Once he had dinner on the go, Seamus handed one cup of tea to her, and taking the other, he went to sit on his own bedroll nest. 'Are you feeling a little warmer?' he asked, and she nodded.

She had stopped shivering, and her hands and feet no longer felt like blocks of ice, but she was still a little cold. She hoped the tea would help warm her, and it did.

They were silent as they waited for the meal to cook. Seamus looked lost in his thoughts and Aliah was too tired to even think of a topic of conversation. Without Amelia to fill in the gaps they seemed to have little to talk about. The only sound in the cave came from the wind, rain, and hail outside the entrance.

When they had finished a passable meal and banked

the fire for the night, the two weary travellers were happy to curl up in their bedrolls and sleep while the storm raged on outside. Aliah awoke the next morning expecting the storm to have passed over only to find it was raging as loud as the night before. She pulled on her waterproof coat and slipped out the door to relieve herself, and found a now white landscape. She hurriedly completed her task and slipped back inside, starting the fire going as much to get warm as to make some porridge for breakfast.

After they finished eating and cleaned up, Seamus went outside to gather some snow in one of their pots to melt. 'We do not know how long this storm will go on so we had best make our water last,' he said.

'Ever the practical one,' Aliah said under her breath as he left, but she was really quite pleased he seemed to know what he was doing. She had never had to survive in the outdoors before, and without his help she would have actually been lost. Even though she hated to admit she needed him.

With breakfast tasks done, they faced a long and boring day as the storm waged on around them. Aliah tried conversation.

'Do you have any brothers and sisters?' she asked.

'A younger brother and sister.' A long pause. 'You?'

'A sister. Younger.' Another long pause.

'Do you miss your sister?'

'No, Bela is not like me at all,' Aliah answered, although she did think to herself, *I miss my mother, even though she has been dead these last four years. And I worry about my father. He did not want to let me go, but he had no choice! If only he knew I was all right and on my way back to him.* But she said none of this to Seamus.

Instead she asked, 'Do you miss your family?'

'Yes.' Then after a pause, 'But it does not do to dwell on it as it is unlikely I will see any of them again.'

And on the day went. They found out more about each other in fits and starts. Seamus did not mind hunting, but would rather ride or read. He preferred eating with his friends in the kitchens rather than in the formal great hall where the heir was expected to show himself. How he had fought to be able to learn how to use knives and bows rather than a sword, which he had no flair for, even though it was known men in his family were quite handy with those forms of weapon.

In return Aliah admitted she was better at fighting and swordsmanship than she was at cooking and sewing. She did not mind reading, but wanted to be able to choose her own reading material. One of the things she and Seamus did have in common was a love of riding as they could both escape their daily chores and be who they wanted on the back of a horse. If Seamus found it odd that her pastimes were more in line with a lady than someone who had been sold to sailors, he did not comment.

During the day, Aliah developed a bit of a cough, which was made a little better by putting some dried sage leaves from Amelia's medicinal pack into her tea. That night the forced inactivity made it difficult to sleep and every time Aliah did doze off her coughing woke her. Eventually she drifted into a fitful slumber.

The next day was much the same as the day before, until some time after noon the wind died down and Seamus went to check what was going on outside. 'It looks as though the storm has passed,' he said on his return. 'But the sky is still very black. I suggest we wait until morning to move off, just to make sure the storm has really passed us by.'

'I suppose that is the sensible thing to do,' Aliah responded.

They spent another restless night. Aliah's cough was no better, but she took heart from the fact it was no worse either.

When they awoke the next morning they dressed for travel and while Aliah cleaned the cave, making it ready for the next travellers who needed it, Seamus went out to find the main track and make sure the snow had cleared enough over night. While she waited for Seamus to return, she stacked the unused wood at the back of the cave and bound some tinder round the torch pole, leaving it in the gap by the door next to the tinderbox.

Seamus returned with a smile on his face. 'The path to the pass has very little snow, it seems the wind has blown it away. Unfortunately, the wind is a little bracing, so we should put our waterproofs on. Other than that we are good to leave.'

6
MOUNTAINS, MOUNTAINS, AND MORE MOUNTAINS

Seamus was grateful to be out of the cave, but he had to admit the wind was a little more bracing on the exposed mountain pass than he would have liked. He estimated if they made good time they would be able to camp on this side of the pass that night, and by noon tomorrow they would be over the pass and walking in the shelter of the mountains the following day. If his map was right, he estimated they would have a further three to four days walk to Sunnydale, depending on their pace.

Anxious to get as close to the pass as possible that day, Seamus set a cracking pace. After the first candle-mark or so, he had to slow as Aliah was struggling to keep up and her breathing sounded a little shallow. The slower pace helped a little, but he did not like the look of sweat on her brow. It looked more like a fever sweat than sweat from walking. However Aliah insisted she was not ailing and urged him to keep going.

As the day drew on and they neared the pass, Seamus began to look out for some suitable shelter for the night. If he were alone he might just have slept in one of the small copse of trees by the road, but Aliah's cough had come back and he wanted to find something with a little more shelter so he could ensure she was not too exposed to the elements during the night.

Finally he found a rocky outcrop with a depression wide enough for the both of them to sleep. It was sheltered from the wind and there was even some scrubby wood close by for a fire. It was a little early to stop, but he decided that they needed to be cautious as neither of them could afford to get really sick.

They set the fire and made a hearty stew for supper. Seamus noticed their supplies were running a little low. They had hoped to be nearer to Sunnydale where they could top their supplies up. But they still had a way to go. They would have to start reducing what they ate, or looking for food on the way once they traversed the pass.

Aliah's cough seemed to settle with some sage tea, and he noticed she added a little dried garlic, so she must have been feeling worse. Monitoring her sleep long into the night, he was concerned she really was not well.

BEGINNINGS

When they woke the next morning Aliah was not coughing as much. After checking she was up to it Seamus had them walking at a brisk pace. As they came closer to the top of the pass the air thinned and it was hard for him to breathe, so it must have been agony for Aliah.

Higher up, the wind grew stronger, and Aliah had to hold fast to Seamus' pack to keep from being blown off the path. He encouraged her to keep going as when they dipped below the pass the wind would not affect her so much. It would not be long now he said. But after the tenth time of him saying it, her eyes began to glaze over and she no longer looked as though she believed him.

It seemed like an eternity, but finally they crested the top of the mountain. Seamus took some time to look down on the rolling hills that finally flattened out towards a town he could just see in the distance. He would have loved more time to take in the view and get his bearings, but Aliah was fading fast. He took in just enough to feel relieved the passage down seemed shorter than the one up, then they started their descent.

As they moved down into the shelter of the mountain the biting wind lessened, but they still had to watch their footing on the patches of ice. It was not yet getting dark, but Seamus began scouting for a sheltered place to make camp, somewhere he might find something to scavenge to supplement their dwindling supplies.

He did not like the shallow sound of Aliah's breathing, and was relieved when he found a rocky outcrop with a half-cave. The floor was dry and there was plenty of wood around, which he quickly gathered. They used tinder from their packs to start the fire, and Seamus left Aliah to begin a stew and brew some tea while he went to see if he could find some additional food.

They were still quite high in the mountains and the weather had taken a turn for the worse. Winter was definitely in the air. That meant there would be little to hunt apart from the cross between lowland rabbits and rats that the locals called mountain rats. He looked around for what could be a likely burrow entrance, somewhere without too much ice around. Just as he was about to give up, he spied a mountain rat darting back into a hole. Looking around, he found the back entrance. He placed the bag he had brought with him over it. At the front entrance he started a small fire, making sure the smoke went into the burrow, then went back to the bag and waited. Before too long he had two mountain rats in his bag. He prepared their meat, then buried the skins and debris before taking his catch back to camp.

Aliah had made tea and fallen asleep while he hunted. There was a pot on the edge of the fire with some dried vegetables and pulses mixed in, with a little of their precious water. Seamus added the meat to the pot and set it over the fire to simmer. He picked up the teapot and took it outside to gather some snow to melt for tomorrow. Finally he rolled out his bedding and leaned back to wait for dinner to finish cooking.

He would have dosed off himself had he not been concerned about the rattling he could hear in Aliah's chest. It was true she was not coughing as much but she was not breathing easily either, and her face had an unhealthy grey pallor. It was almost a shame to wake her so she could eat some stew.

BEGINNINGS

After dinner he fed her some more tea, then let her go back to sleep while he tidied everything up and made ready for the next day. All the time he was thinking to himself thank goodness it is only four more days at most until Sunnydale.

That was what he kept repeating to himself for the next three days as they made slow progress due to Aliah's failing health. He repeated it when they took a turning and walked half a day in the wrong direction, then had to walk back. He repeated it when Aliah had to stop every few paces to get her breath. He repeated it when he put down both packs and eased his aching shoulders at night.

Each day they were covering less and less distance, and their food supplies were running perilously low. It took them more than the planned two days to get to the bottom of the pass, and by then, Seamus was exhausted. He had been carrying Aliah's pack and supporting most of her weight for the best part of the last three days.

On the fourth day they finally emerged from the foothills onto the flat. Seamus set up camp for the night by the side of the road under the shelter of a large Elm tree. Aliah had collapsed as soon as they stopped walking, so he unpacked her bedding and made sure she was warm so she could sleep. He then set up the fire and started a broth with left over meat from the day before, and made a medicinal tea for her. At least water was not a problem with all the ice still around. Food, however, was another matter. There was barely enough for breakfast, and at normal walking pace they still had about two days to Sunnydale. They would have to stop at a farm and see if they could buy some food.

While he fed Aliah the tea to bring down her fever and help her chest, he tried not to let on how worried he was about her condition, or how far they were from their first destination. 'We will be in Sunnydale soon,' he told her, but did not add he had no idea how they were going to make it that far. Seamus drank his broth, then forced Aliah to have some before banking up the fire and crawling into his own blankets. Although he was worried about how they were going to actually make it to the town, he was so exhausted he fell asleep almost before his head touched the ground.

He awoke before dawn the next morning unable to sleep any longer. Checking on Aliah he found her much worse. Her face was flushed, and she was breathing shallowly through half-parted lips. She would not wake when he shook her, and her fever was really high. Seamus knew if they continued walking for two days to Sunnydale, Aliah might not make it there.

Going through his options he busied himself with stoking up the fire and making tea. He waited for the sun to rise so he could have a look around and see if there was anywhere he could get help. In the distance he could just make out a farmhouse. He did not have much money, but maybe he could "borrow" a horse and take Aliah to town that way. He would return it later.

Making sure Aliah was well tucked in and the fire would burn for a while, he headed for the house at a slow jog. It seemed like candle-marks later, but really it was not even one, when he arrived at the farm just as the farmer was heading out of his cottage. He nearly scared the man half to death as he came up behind him. In fact, the farmer had scared him also, and Seamus realised he would not be able to borrow the horse as planned.

'Do not be scaring me like that, young sir,' the startled farmer grumbled. 'It is quiet in these parts, and normally somebody coming up that fast behind a soul does not have good intentions.'

Thinking on his feet Seamus said, 'I am sorry, sir, but I am in kind of a rush. I have been travelling with my sister who has fallen sick. I need to get her to a healer in Sunnydale. I was wondering if I could rent a horse and cart to take her?' Seamus managed to get his request out between panting breaths.

'I would be a trusting soul if I just let you take off with my horse and cart.' The man screwed up his face in thought. 'But the goddess would look poorly on me if you were indeed an honest soul with a sick friend and I did nothing.' Seamus looked at the man in what he hoped was a beseeching way, willing him to help.

'And I would never forgive you either.' The door opened and there stood a woman about the age of the farmer, although much shorter. 'Jon, why not take the boy back to his friend and you can decide whether or not he is honest then and there.' Her shrewd eyes bored through Seamus. 'I assume you have real coin to pay?'

It was like she was looking into Seamus' very soul, and it made him more than a little uncomfortable. Here was a woman you would not cross lightly. He put on his best "trust me I am honest" face, the one designed to get adults to agree to let him have something when he really should not, and pulled out his purse. Hearing the coins tinkle, the woman nodded to her husband, then spoke to Seamus.

'Go and help Jon hitch up the horse, then. Sooner he gets to your friend the better.'

Seamus followed the man to the barn where there was a rather fine looking horse and a beat up cart. He helped the farmer get the cart ready to go. When they were done he also helped the farmer load some baskets of potatoes and root vegetables onto the back. Jon included an old horse blanket.

'If I be going into town I may as well get the most out of the journey.' The man chuckled as he loaded the cart. 'I will need to make up for not working today.'

Guilt welled up, but then Seamus shook it off. His first thought had been he might steal a horse and return it later. At least this way the farmer would get paid for his time.

As they left the barn the farmer's wife came out. 'You seem true of heart young man, but just beware if anything happens to my Jon. I have seen your face and I will make sure you are hunted down.'

Seamus was sure she would hunt him to the grave, but Jon chuckled beside him. 'Her bark is worse than her bite,' he said. 'Heart of gold, my Maisie, but you would not want to cross her.' And with one last chuckle they were off.

Worrying all the way back about what he would find, Seamus was even more concerned than he had been when he left. Aliah had not moved in his absence and her temperature seemed to be even higher, if that were even possible.

'She's not looking too well,' Jon offered helpfully.

'I have some herbs in my pack, I will make her some tea and it will ease her breathing a little.'

BEGINNINGS

'I think she be needing a healer, not tea,' the farmer commented sagely. 'We best get her on the cart and get going as soon as possible.'

Seamus frowned and bit his lip, considering his best course of action. He voiced his agreement and began rolling up his bedding and packing their packs. All the while he explained to Aliah what was happening in the hopes she would be able to hear him. Jon helped him to place Aliah in the back of the cart and they both made sure she was warmly covered before Seamus put out their fire, buried their rubbish, stowed their packs and joined Jon on the wagon bench.

'Away ye go, Mabel.' Jon started them off, and some of the tension Seamus had felt for the last few days left his body.

7
CASTLE DREAMS

As she half-woke Aliah imagined a stranger was carrying her. An older man with a weathered face and a woollen hat pulled down on his head. But she forgot him as soon as she closed her eyes and started to drift off again. Her throat was so closed up she could barely breathe, her body was full of aches and pains, and her skin was on fire. There was a great pressure on her chest, like someone was sitting on her.

In some part of her mind she knew they would have

to be on their way soon and she should be helping Seamus to break camp, but try as she might she could not will her body to move. She was not sure how she was going to walk at all today.

Drifting back off to sleep Aliah found herself back home. She was riding her horse, running and playing with her friends, and even doing her lessons with the court scribes. In some part of her mind she realised her body was being shifted from beside the fire, but she was too engrossed in living her life in the castle to take much notice. And soon she was being rocked back to sleep.

At some time during her ride Aliah began to feel cold and asked one of the grooms for a cloak. The rocking was encouraging her to sleep, but she was chilled to the bone even with the sun on her face. The rocking stopped and a voice penetrated her consciousness. She could not quite place it. The name Seamus popped into her head. He helped her drink water. There was some rummaging. Then she was a little warmer. The rocking started and she fell asleep again.

Her sleep was not as comfortable this time. She was back in the castle, but she was watching her father read a letter handed to him by the captain of a foreign ship. From the look on his face it was not good news. In fact, she would say it was extremely bad news. Then all hell broke loose. Her father ordered the guard to seize the ship's captain and his crew, and he stormed out of the throne room. The court broke for the day, and Aliah's governess grabbed her by the arm and escorted her back to her room and sternly told her, 'For once in your life, stay here as you are bid. I do not like the sound of what

BEGINNINGS

has been happening and your safety is paramount.'

During the session of her father's court Aliah had been deep in a conversation with her guard about the chance of a ride after the session was finished. As such, she missed the captain's entrance and the conversation that occurred before he handed over the sealed letter. It meant she had no idea why Mistress Narinda was so concerned about her safety, and she was not going to waste such a beautiful afternoon in her room. However, try as she might, she could not find anyone to escort her riding. No matter how much she wheedled they all turned her down, more worried about her father's wrath than normal.

In the end she had no choice but to obey her governess' command and return to her room. In the end it was a good thing no one had given in to her, as she was summoned to her father's rooms just as the dinner bell was due to ring. Dressing herself with special care, she allowed her governess to tie her hair back in a plait without complaint.

The guards admitted her immediately, and she was dismayed to see her father's mood did not appear any better than it had been earlier in the day. He curtly told her to take a seat by the fire while his squire finished dressing him. When her father was fully dressed in a brilliant blue doublet and dark blue hose the squire was dismissed and her father took the chair opposite her, on the other side of the fire.

'Aliah, I do not know where to start.' He brushed his hand through his curly, greying, dark hair. A frown creased his brow. 'I am going to have to ask you to be very grown up, more grown up than I have ever asked of you before.'

Aliah shifted uncomfortably in her seat as her father's grey eyes stared directly at her. She had only recently been included in court sessions and she found those boring. What more could her father ask of her? Still, she stared back at him, hoping her blue eyes conveyed an interest she did not really feel. 'Go ahead, father.'

'You will know from attending court that we have been approached by a nation across the sea, Carsten. Initially they were proposing a trade alliance. However, just recently their missives have been more strongly worded, and it has become apparent they did not want to partner with us, but want us to become a client state within a Carsten Empire. As our ties have always been with the Natari Emperor, we have been strongly resisting their advances.'

She knew that if she had been paying attention at sessions of the court, she would have noticed. But normally, when forced to attend, she found something else to occupy her time while her father was busy discussing matters of state. In her defence, the rules of state decreed she could never hold the Crown of Aria, that duty would fall to her husband, but she would have a seat at the Council table. That was why she was included in all important discussions. Aliah was beginning to wish she had taken her duties as potential heir a little more seriously. She nodded at her father to continue as if she knew exactly what he was talking about.

'We have appealed to the Natari Emperor for support should this state become hostile, but it appears our two nations have drifted so far apart we are no longer considered to be part of their national responsibility. Add to that a war on their eastern border which has gained their full attention and we are left on our own to deal with Carsten.' King Terion stood and began pacing the room. Aliah's brow creased as she realised the country could be in danger from a threat she had not even known about.

'Our nation is fragmented. Two of our five Duchies would be unlikely to support an all out war, and what intelligence our spies have gleaned, lead them to advise us not to antagonise the Carstenites as we may not like the results. They are a strong warrior nation and would take any opportunity to begin a war. That has placed us in a very weak position.'

Her father sat again and picked up a goblet of wine from the table between them. 'And this is what we are brought to.' He sighed. 'I don't like it, but I cannot see any way out of it.'

Terion leaned forward and took his daughter's hand, 'Their king, Spearon, has demanded the hand of my eldest daughter. If I refuse, there is no doubt in my mind he will invade our country.'

Aliah froze. 'Eldest daughter?'

'But surely you cannot give in to this man. You always told me if you give in once to a bully you are leaving yourself open to be bullied again,' Aliah spluttered as she tried to gather her thoughts.

'I am sorry, my darling, matters of state are a little different to courtyard politics. We, my advisors and I, can see no way around his request at this time. It is not as if you did not know that your marriage would be arranged to benefit the state.' He stroked her hand, but Aliah would not meet his eyes. She was frowning and it was like a dark cloud had crossed her face.

'Yes,' she ground out through clenched teeth. 'But mother always said that I was to marry someone who could help rule the Kingdom and consolidate the Duchies behind the throne. And that I would have some say in who that person was. It never meant marriage to a foreigner WHOM I HAVE NEVER MET!' She stood up and began pacing the room, her anger making it impossible to sit still.

Terion folded his daughter in his arms. 'I know, my love, and that was what we both wished for you. But I can see no other way around this, much as I dislike it on so many levels. As rulers of this land we hold a position of privilege, and in return, it is our responsibility to live our lives for our people. I hate that I am to ask this of you, but I am asking anyway. It will be of little consolation to you that Spearon thinks to unite our lands by marrying my heir. But he does not realise that you have not been formally named as Heir, and would not be until your eighteenth birthday. As he only asked for my eldest daughter's hand, not my heir, he will not be getting exactly what he bargained for.'

'I am glad you are so pleased with yourselves!' Aliah looked him in the eye, wanting him to see how hurt and angry she was at what he was asking. 'Such a small price to pay for you, but what will happen to me once he realises?'

'I do not know,' her father sadly acknowledged, and her heart melted a little as she could see the concern in his face. 'But I trust you will be able to look after yourself in any situation, and I am sending an advisor with you who is one of my best-trained wizards. He should be able to protect you in most situations. He will also enable you to communicate with us whenever you need. And it is no small price that I pay by letting you go. I appreciate that I am also asking much of you. If I could find another way ...'

Aliah tossed and turned in her sleep, alternating between shivering cold and a raging fever, not sure whether she was restless from her illness or from her tortured memories. In some part of her mind she noticed the rocking had stopped, and there were many people talking. Then she was back in the castle with so many people getting her ready to depart to her new life, trying to persuade her she was doing the right thing for her country. She gave herself over to their ministrations feeling dead inside. All too soon she was saying a tearful farewell to her father and sister and boarding the ship with her governess and advisor.

For the first part of her trip she was treated as a queen. Then at the first port Narinda and Servious were forced from the ship and left behind. After that Aliah was locked in her cabin. It seemed that women in Carsten were deemed little better than cattle, even those who were destined to become queen. The more Aliah learned, the more she realised her father had no idea what he was getting her in to. She overheard the captain saying, 'Once she meets her future king that little wench will get her comcuppance.' He would use her as a symbol of how weak the mainlanders were to rally his troops to war. If the comments of her captors were to be believed, rather than stopping a war, her marriage would be used to start one. Aliah realised she had to get away and inform her father, and she needed to do it quietly, before his advisors could talk him into returning her to her dreaded fate.

However, they had not only locked her in her cabin, they tied her up. She struggled, trying to get free from her bonds, sleeping when she could to get the strength to struggle again. She would break free. Whatever it took she must get home. It must be mealtime as she could smell meat cooking and, strangely, sunshine on her face.

Aliah forced her eyes opened and was surprised to see not a sailor, but Seamus smiling down at her.

'You were right, she was waking,' he said to someone over his shoulder.

She raised her head a little, surprised to see that they were in a simple, but clean house. She was in a bed and Seamus was sitting on a chair beside her. Behind him she could just make a figure by the fire. Struggling to get her mind around walking on the road, escaping ship, and being here—wherever it was—Aliah turned to the one person she recognised: Seamus.

'It's all right. We are in Sunnydale, Ali,' he said as he gently lifted her head and fed her some broth from a spoon. 'We have been here a six-day. Drink this and rest some more. I will catch you up on everything later.'

Exhausted after a few spoonfuls of broth, Aliah was pleased to lie back down and close her eyes. This time the sleep she drifted into was dreamless and healing.

8
SUNNYDALE

Seamus sat by Aliah's bedside through the night. Each time she woke he fed her a little more broth. She would go back to sleep and he would doze in the chair for a while. He was so relieved she was no longer thrashing around the bed, nor did she appear to be running a fever. Healer Goodwyn had done a good job treating what she called a breathing sickness.

When they arrived at the Healer's house, Aliah's breathing was laboured and she had been flushed bright red with fever. Healer Goodwyn took them in, saying it would take time, but his sister, Ali, was young and strong and with rest and the right medication she would get better. She stressed the time element, saying these things could not be rushed. But time was not something they could spare, nor did they have enough money to pay for care and accommodation for any length of time.

Seamus was honest with the healer. He had very little coin left after paying for their transport, and they needed to be somewhere very soon. Having explained their situation he thanked her for her time and offered to pay her what little coin he had left for some herbs. The healer may have been elderly, but she was still strong of heart, and she showed him that it was the nature of most people to help those less well off. She shushed him.

'I have enough coin for my needs thanks to my late husband. What I do not have are a strong back and young legs. You can contribute to the household by preparing the garden for winter for me, and there are repairs I need around the house. Local gossip is that the blacksmith's apprentice has hurt his leg and he might need some extra help. So you might earn some coin for your and your sister's food.

'Bring that girl in here,' she commanded Jon.

Shrugging his shoulders Jon headed to the cart. 'You best mind a woman when they speak to yer like that,' he told Seamus as he helped bring Aliah into the house. When they were settled Jon exclaimed he best be off; he did not want to be back too late as his missus was a bit of a worrier. Seamus had thanked him for his help, feeling a little guilty that he had considered stealing from the man.

'You mind the healer, she will help you look after that

BEGINNINGS

sister of yours,' Jon yelled over his shoulder as he departed.

For two days, Seamus had stuck close to the healer's house, and Aliah. He repaired a broken shutter and a storage cupboard, then prepared her extensive garden for winter. In addition he tended to the herbs that were hardy enough to stand the early winter cold. That done, he chopped enough wood for at least two winters and stacked it in the lean-to beside the house. Finally, Healer Goodwin set him out in the direction of the Blacksmith's place, declaring his sister would not heal any faster for his moping around and he might as well make use of his time in Sunnydale to put some coin back in his purse.

The blacksmith was a large, hearty man with a ready grin and shock of wavy black hair. He had looked Seamus up and down, declaring him a little skinny, which made Seamus glower. Thankfully he was more than pleased to have whatever help was on offer. It seemed his apprentice had twisted his ankle a six-day before and still could only just bear weight. Many farmers had bought their equipment in for repair with the sudden change of weather and there was a pile of jobs backing up. He set Seamus to work straight away keeping the fire going, fetching and carrying and cleaning. The smith kept him pretty busy for the next few days, working long into the evening to try and clear the backlog of work.

The manual work in the blacksmith's shop tired him out as he was not used to constant physical labour, but still he kept vigil by Aliah's bedside during the night. Watching and waiting patiently for her to wake long enough so he could remind her of their cover story. While he was pleased she no longer breathed so heavily, and he trusted Healer Goodwin and Smith Brown, he did not want to take needless chances with Aliah blurting out the wrong thing as she awoke. Still, he could not stay awake forever, and not long before dawn he was started awake by a hand on his arm.

'Shh,' Aliah said, finger over her lips, 'I can see a woman asleep and I don't want to wake her.'

'Ali, you're awake. It's me, Sean,' he whispered back, nodding at her and then towards the figure sleeping in the room on the other side of the fire.

'I know who we are, numbskull! I have not lost my wits.' Aliah smiled to take the sting out of her words. 'Where are we? How long have we been here?' Aliah whispered.

'We're in Sunnydale,' Seamus whispered back. 'I paid a farmer to bring us here. We have been here for just over a six-day.'

'That long?' Aliah's face crumpled in dismay.

'And Healer Goodwin, who took us in, says it will be another six-day after you wake up before we can travel.'

'Twelve days?' she asked. 'We have lost so much time because of me!' Her brow creased in a frown.

Surprised, Seamus looked at Aliah. He knew she wanted to reach home as quickly as possible to tell the King of the potential war, but he had not realised it would bother her quite so much. 'Time?' he asked her, raising his eyebrows questioningly. Was she playing her part and appearing to worry about the delay in meeting her future husband? Or was there more to it?

'How can we have been here so long? We had so little money.' She ignored his question and asked her own. He noticed she had a tendency to do that when she was focused on something else.

'The healer has looked after us and I have done some work for her in return. I have also been working for the blacksmith,' Seamus said, rather proudly, for it was the first time he had ever actually been paid for his labour. But he could tell by Aliah's gaze she had moved on to something else. He tried to get her attention back. 'We now have a little more coin than when we started. We may even be able to afford to take a coach part of the way.'

There was a noise behind them, and it was Seamus' turn to put his finger to his lips. 'We'll talk more later,' he said. 'Go back to sleep. I have to get ready for work. Healer Goodwin will look after you.' He gestured to the elderly woman sleeping in the other bed. 'I will see you this evening.' If he noticed the frown on Aliah's face as he closed down any further discussion, he chose to ignore it.

Seamus had a quick breakfast, checked Aliah was asleep, then headed to work. The day dragged on as if it would never end, and to make it worse, his mind was not on the job. When he let the fire go too low for the third time that day, Smith Brown told him to go as he was not much help anyway. Promising to do better tomorrow, Seamus ran like the wind back to the healer's house.

He rushed through the door expecting to see Aliah

still in bed, but the house was empty. Nothing looked disturbed. Although he was worried, he decided not to panic. He stoked the fire and put the stew pot over the flames readying it for dinner before going outside to wash up. As he was changing into clean clothes, the cottage door opened. Aliah came in, fully dressed, leaning on Healer Goodwin, who was taking the strain well given she was a head shorter than her charge. Although she looked pale and drawn, Aliah seemed better than she had in many days.

'Sean, you are home already.' She seemed genuinely pleased to see him. 'Goodwin took me to the baths. She said a good soak would help me feel better, and it did. But I became tired on the way back.' Healer Goodwin helped her to the bed, and it was then that Seamus noticed the child standing by the door.

'I won't be a moment,' Healer Goodwin said to him. 'Just let me get my things and I will come with you.' To Seamus she said, 'Henry's mother is having her baby and needs my help. You see Ali back into bed, and make sure you and she have some supper. Keep some warm for me as I do not know when I will be back. Babies do not come to any plan.' She shuffled off to her back room, and emerged a few minutes later with a bag in one hand and a glass vial in the other.

'Give Ali half of this after she has eaten. It will help with her breathing, and also make her drowsy. She needs a good nights sleep to help the healing process along. If she wakes during the night she may have the other half.' And with that, Healer Goodwin followed Henry out the door and they were alone.

BEGINNINGS

Seamus went to help Aliah into bed, but she waved him away. 'I shall be fine, if you would just turn your back.' He did, and a few minutes later she said, 'All right, I am presentable now.'

Aliah was propped up in her bed, wearing her tunic, her skirt was draped neatly over the end of the bed. 'So, what is for dinner?'

'Dinner will still be a little while, so we should take this opportunity to talk. We don't know how long Goodwin will be. As she said, babies can be unpredictable.' Seamus pulled over a chair and sat beside her. 'We need to make some plans, and I also think from some of the things you said while you were feverish, that you have not been very straight with me.' Seamus put on a stern face and looked her straight in the eye.

Aliah looked confused but met his stare straight on, giving nothing away. He pressed on. 'While you were in a fever you spoke of King Terion, and your father, and of Millard, who I know to be one of the king's advisors. You spoke the names of some of the Kingdom's most influential people and then said you must tell father. You kept repeating that phrase, *I must tell father there is danger coming.*' Seamus paused, waiting expectantly, but this time Aliah would not meet his eyes.

'And now you are very concerned that so much time passed while you were getting better. Is there something you would like to tell me? Or should I guess just what position your family has held in Castle Bannock, Princess Aliahanna?' He almost enjoyed seeing the shocked expression on her face, but it confirmed his worst fear. He had been travelling with the Heir to the Throne of Aria. Before they had only faced minor danger, but now he was caught up in something much larger and much scarier, an actual potential invasion of his homeland. And he might well be travelling with the very reason for it.

'I guess it is time I shared my burden with someone.' Aliah sighed, clearly wishing she did not have to tell him anything at all, which annoyed Seamus immensely. He had always been straight with her—well, at least since Amelia had outed him—but before he could say anything along those lines, Aliah carried on speaking.

'It is only fair you know what you are getting yourself into before we travel any further together.' She looked so serious and so worried that Seamus bit back his sarcastic comment and listened.

Some time later Aliah had told her story and they had eaten dinner. 'So you can see why I am worried about this delay.' She finished her recount. 'I need to get word to my father as soon as possible, and I need to do it without alerting his advisors.'

Seamus had been thinking things through as Aliah was talking, and he had a plan. He just had to see if he could convince Aliah it was the best course to take. And with her need for speed, it would not be an easy proposition.

'Firstly,' he said. 'Would you agree that you cannot just walk into the palace as Princess Aliahanna?'

'Yes,' Aliah confirmed.

'And secondly, there has been no sign of any invasion as we would have heard something in the days we have been in town.'

'That is true,' she answered. 'But that does not mean one is still not imminent.'

BEGINNINGS

'Agreed, but it does mean we still have a little time. And, finally, one thing has not changed; we need to be careful as we travel as my family is looking for me. On top of that, there is nothing to say that your captors are not still looking for you.'

Aliah nodded.

'So, I have been doing some research while you have been sleeping.'

'Sleeping! A little bit of an understatement,' Aliah laughed and Seamus grinned at her attempt at humour.

'I have been asked to help drive one of the wagons on a trading trip to Duncameron. The smith's boy is travelling to meet his family there and will be well enough to drive the wagon back but they need someone to drive it there. That leaves in two days time. I do not think you will be well enough to travel by then.

'I had also thought to use some of our coin to take the coach to Port Isby and then maybe catch a ship from there. But the coach leaves tomorrow, and I think it is out of the question now for the same reason. We could take the one in six days, but I think my final option is better.

'If we stay here another six-day, I think I can earn enough for a small horse and still be able to top up our supplies. If you rode, we could start out within a next six-day, and head inland towards Duncameron. And from there, follow the inland road to Bannock. We still remain undetected and reach there quicker than going via Port Isby.'

Aliah's brow furrowed and her face clouded. 'Even if we move quickly, Duncameron is just under six-days walk away, and then it would be *another* six-day until we reached the Castle. In twelve days we could be facing a full-scale invasion, without the country being prepared.'

'I had a feeling you might say that, and I think you are wrong to believe your father does not at least have some idea of what is going on. After all, I understand he has quite a large spy network as he likes to keep his finger on the pulse of the nation. And at least this way, we have a chance of getting to see him before the invasion. If we get caught then we have no chance.' Seamus stood up and stretched. 'Anyway, we do not have to decide now. You will not be ready to travel for days yet.' He handed her the medicine Healer Goodwin had left. 'Let me carry on looking into all the possibilities, and we can decide what to do when the healer says you are fit to travel.'

'I know you are just putting me off, but I am too tired to bother arguing with you,' Aliah said tucking a stray piece of hair behind her ear as she snuggled into bed. 'Never fear, we WILL talk about it later, and I WILL be doing some looking myself.' She drifted off, still frowning her displeasure.

Seamus pulled his pallet out from under Aliah's bed and prepared to get some sleep himself. He knew things were now more tangled than they had been, more fraught with danger. But he was strangely calmer, not more stressed, for having his fears confirmed. At least now he knew what he was facing, and Aliah did not seem all that imperious for a royal princess. Well, not while she was still ill anyway. Although she did seem quite annoyed with him about something. Well, they could sort that out later. He fell asleep still going through a list of all the things he had to do to get them ready to leave for Duncameron.

BEGINNINGS

The following morning, Aliah waited for the sound of the door closing, signalling Seamus was heading off to work. Through half-opened eyes she could see the outline of Healer Goodwyn asleep in her bed through the open door to her room. Without the need to arise, she took the opportunity to snuggle beneath the covers and think through everything she and Seamus had discussed last night.

Seamus had seemed so certain of what they should do, but that was so like him. Aliah was not so sure they had the luxury of time, and she was going to do something about that. It had already been more than two six-days since she had escaped captivity. More than enough time for her captors to return to Carsten to recruit a small army. Soldiers could be leaving any day now and her father needed as much time as possible to prepare to meet them. Gathering a large army took time. This much she had learned from attending her father's council.

Although it pained her to agree with Seamus, he had been right that she was in no fit state to walk, or even to ride anywhere, if they left now. So that meant taking the coach, which left today, or joining the caravan leaving tomorrow. She did not know if she had enough for the coach trip, that meant the caravan was her best option. Would they take her even though she was unwell? Whatever she did, she knew she had to be on her way. She was not waiting another six-day.

Unable to find a solution, Aliah dozed off again. She

was woken a little time later by the sound of Healer Goodwyn moving around. Drowsily she sat up, surprised that she was feeling quite a bit better than she had the day before.

'Oh, good,' her healer said. 'You are awake. Are you ready to try some of the morning out of bed?' She placed a pot of porridge over the fire.

'I think so,' Aliah responded. 'I am certainly keen to be moving.' She sat up and reached for her top and skirt, then tucked her feet into her indoor shoes.

'Not too much too fast though,' Healer Goodwyn admonished. 'I know you are probably very eager to be on your way to meet with your betrothed, but you have been quite ill. It will take some time for your body to repair. Maybe the morning up and about, then rest this afternoon.' She bustled about getting honey and dried fruit for breakfast and placed them on the table.

'Both Sean and I appreciate all your help, but we really would like to be on our way as soon as possible.' Aliah cleaned her face and hands in the basin of water Goodwyn left for her on the bench by the door.

'You cannot be walking and riding for some time, I fear,' Goodwyn told her as she brought the pot of oat porridge to the table and ladled some into the two waiting plates. 'I know you feel good now, but by the afternoon you will feel very tired. If you leave here too early you would undo all the good work I have done healing you, and you would not be a very welcome sight for your betrothed.' She placed the pan on the stove then sat at the table.

Aliah sat down, frowning. That was almost exactly what Seamus had said, and it was not what she really wanted to hear. 'My betrothed and his family will be worried. They will be expecting us any day now. I don't want to cause them any unnecessary concerns, or have them think I am not sturdy enough for their son.' She hoped that would be something a real betrothed country girl would worry about.

'I can understand that. If only you had been travelling by cart you could have left a mite earlier as it would not be such a strain on you. Especially as you are only travelling to the other side of Duncameron. It would only be two, probably three days at this time of year.' She pushed a bowl towards Aliah. 'No mind. Best eat your breakfast,' she finished as she added fruit and honey to her own bowl of porridge and began eating.

They ate in silence. Aliah helped clear the table and wash the dishes, then they spent some time preparing a simple meat stew for dinner. When they were done Goodwyn asked if she would like to help her bottle and store some of the herbs she had collected and dried hanging from the ceiling in her store-room. Aliah said she would and followed Goodwin into the small room where she prepared and stored her herbs and medicines.

'While you do that, I might just make up some more of your medicine.' The healer set Aliah at the main table and retired to her room to work.

The rest of the morning passed quickly as Aliah was kept busy, but she could not get her mind off the thought that it was only two or three days to Duncameron by cart. From there, only another three days to Bannock by cart. She could be home in a six-day. She was sure they could not afford a cart, but there was a caravan leaving and it would only take a little longer.

'Healer Goodwyn?'

'Mmm?'

'Is there any coach or the like to Duncameron?' she asked.

'No, my dear, most folk around here have no reason to go there, and they certainly would not want to come to a small village like this!'

'Oh.'

'But you can get a coach to Port Isby and then a coach to Duncameron. It takes about a six-day or so.'

'Oh, maybe I will talk to Sean about that.' Aliah made her best "I am going to do the right thing" face for Goodwin. Really she was thinking the opposite. *It was way too long going by coach, the caravan was still the best option.*

'Your betrothed is a lucky man to be getting such a smart wife.' Goodwin looked approvingly at her. 'I can enquire about the cost when I go out later to pick up some supplies if you like.'

'If you would not mind.'

'I tell you what, I will see you settled after the noon-time meal, then I will run my errands.'

Pleased with herself, Aliah continued to measure the herbs and bottle them as instructed. Just before noon, she complained of a tiredness she did not really feel. Healer Goodwyn insisted she take a nap before the midday meal. Explaining she would be out when Aliah awoke, she showed her where she kept the medicine she had made for her, and where there was some bread and cheese for her midday meal.

Crawling into bed Aliah feigned sleep. Healer Goodwin

cleared away her workings, then made and ate her midday meal. A little later she checked Aliah was still sleeping, donned her cloak, and left her home to run errands.

Aliah made herself count to twenty slowly before leaping out of bed. She went into the storeroom and took enough of her medicine for four days. From the pantry, she took enough bread and cheese for the time it would take to get to Duncameron. Feeling guilty, she placed half of her coins down on the table, hoping if it did not cover what she had taken, Seamus would make up the difference. She did not like taking from someone who had been so good to her, but her duty to Aria had to come before any personal feelings.

She packed her travelling pack, dressed in clean clothes, and put on her walking boots. Finally she donned her sword and cloak. She was ready to begin her journey to Bannock, on her terms. Closing the door quietly behind her, she left the safety of Healer Goodwin's to find her own way home.

As a point of pride Seamus made sure he kept his mind on what he was doing all day, even though his thoughts wanted to race away and plan the next part of their journey. Smith Brown was pleased with his work and let him leave early as he needed to sort through what things he wanted to send with the caravan going to Duncameron.

Seamus rushed home, but stopped himself bursting through the door at speed because he did not want to scare Aliah with the noise. But it was he who received the surprise. He opened the door to find Aliah's bed empty and Healer Goodwin sitting in one of the chairs beside the fire looking decidedly angry.

'What has happened?' The question exploded out of Seamus' mouth before he could stop it. 'Where is Ali?'

'I have to say, Sean, I have enjoyed having you in my house, but I cannot say the same of your sister. I have never in my life met such a deceitful girl.' Healer Goodwin rose to her full height, which was not very high at all.

'I arrived home today to find your sister had packed up and left. Took some medicine from me and some bread and cheese. She left some coins, I assume to pay for things she took. No note. Nothing to say thank you. Nothing even for you to tell you where she has gone. Unless she left something in your belongings, I have not checked there. These are not the actions of a good girl going to her betrothed.'

The Healer's words took the wind right out of Seamus. He stood there in the open door not knowing what to do. So many things were going round in his mind he did not know where to start. Seeing he was not in a good way, Goodwin shut the door behind him, took his hand, and led him to the chair on the opposite side of the fire.

'You sit yourself down a minute. I can see this is a shock for you.' She busied herself then handed him a cup of warm tea. 'Here you go, drink that, boy. I let my anger get the better of me. This just does not seem normal.' The elderly woman sat down opposite Seamus, concern now creasing her face.

So many things were going through Seamus' mind. Where had Aliah gone? Why had she left without him?

BEGINNINGS

Had she gone mad? No, she had not gone mad. She had taken medicine and food, so she must have had a plan. He should have realised her worry over getting to her father in time meant she was not prepared to wait. Going over their conversation, he realised she had said as much. But to not even discuss it with him ... Then again, she had already shown a tendency to act first and think later. Should he try and follow her? He really did not know whether he even wanted to. He took a deep breath and found himself face to face with Healer Goodwin.

'Are you all right? You went blank for a while there. I was getting a little concerned.' She sat back down and sipped her tea.

'Sorry.' Seamus shook his head in an effort to clear it. 'I was just thinking. I am so sorry, Healer Goodwin. I have not been quite honest with you. It is true that we were heading to meet my sister's betrothed, what I had not told you is she had never met him before, and was not exactly happy about the arrangement.' Seamus should have been worried at how easily the lie rolled off his tongue. He told himself he was not trying to save Aliah, but was trying to make a stranger who had been kind to him not feel like she had been betrayed, and it was actually closer to the truth than their original story.

'Have you any idea when Ali left?' he asked, hoping to buy some time to decide what he should do.

Goodwin shook her head. 'I left around midday, and returned less than a candle-mark before you did. She was asking about carriage trips today, and I did tell her there was one to Port Isby. She may have taken that, although there is no way of knowing until it returns, unless someone saw her board.'

'If she took a carriage to Port Isby she could be heading home. She did have some coin on her, we split it in case we were robbed.' In his own head, he did think it likely she had taken the carriage. She could easily get to Bannock from Port Isby.

'So will you be following her?'

That was the big question. Seamus was so angry Aliah had not waited for him, after all he had done to help her get this far and get well. He had put his own plans on hold. Even so, he was drawn to follow her. Aria was in danger and as a duke's son he should be doing everything to help the people of the Southern Duchy and Hand. On the other hand, he could no longer return home and he needed to find someone to teach him how to control his magic. He should continue with his plan and head to The Wizard's Isle.

'I would like to follow her, she should not be travelling alone,' Seamus admitted. 'But if she is silly enough to run away then I think she can spend some time travelling by herself to see what it is like. Maybe that will teach her a lesson. I will need to go to Duncameron and let her future family know what has happened and see if I can repair the damage. I think that is what our parents would want.' Seamus tried to look like he imagined a worried brother should look.

'If you are sure. It is dangerous for a girl to travel alone. If you do not follow, you run the risk of never seeing your sister again.' In spite of Aliah's actions, the good-natured healer was still looking out for her best interests.

'I know. After I have been to Duncameron I will head

to Isby and see if I can pick up her trail.'

The healer looked at him carefully for a moment, sighed, then stood up. 'If you are going to Duncameron you may as well take up the offer to drive one of the wagons. That way you can save your pennies for chasing after your sister. You had best be off, and see if you can catch them before they finish for the evening. They will be able to load another wagon now they have an extra driver, and that will take some organising.'

Seamus did not move for a minute, he chewed at his lip and then decided. 'Yes, you are right. I will head to the smithy, they have been loading the wagons in the stables there. Hopefully someone will still be around, if not Smith Brown will know where to find them. I can also tell Smith Brown that I am finishing today. Thank you for being so understanding.' He looked sadly at Healer Goodwin.

'Off with you. I will have supper ready when you return.'

It was not until much later that Seamus arrived back at Healer Goodwin's house. Although his ability to join the team had been treated as a gift from the goddess—even after he had explained he had never driven a team of horses before—there was a lot of work to do to load the third wagon and he had felt obliged to help.

By the time he ate his supper he was ready to drop. He managed to pack his belongings after having checked for, but not found, a message from Aliah. Then he crashed into bed to try and get some sleep before the long journey tomorrow.

9
THE ROAD TO DUNCAMERON

The next morning Healer Goodwyn insisted on walking with Seamus to the blacksmith's stables to see him off. Seamus was genuinely quite sad to say good-bye to her and Smith Brown. Although he would never make a good blacksmith himself, he had enjoyed his first ever paying job and, if his pay was anything to go by, Smith Brown had appreciated his work. Healer Goodwin had opened her home to him and he took pride in helping her over the last six-day. It gave him hope to know he could find some sort of life outside of Hand. It was difficult saying good-bye to them both.

The rest of the travelling party was already outside the stables when they arrived. The head of the group was a seasoned caravan boss everyone simply called, "Boss". He was a large, heavily muscled man with a weathered face that was all stern until he smiled. Then it was like the sun had come out from behind a cloud.

He showed Seamus to his team and Seamus immediately started to get to know the horses. Checking they were tethered correctly, he fed them an apple each to try and make friends. Boss nodded in approval, and Seamus was pleased the tactic he used on new horses in his father's stables was appropriate for working horses.

He was introduced to Boss' daughter, Megan, and her husband, Able. They in turn introduced Seamus to the two guards who would be riding with them as Boss had other things to be getting on with. The guards were both retired soldiers. Grunt was the senior of the two, but it was his companion, Helen, who asked him what he was able to do in case of attack. She was satisfied with Seamus being able to use his knives, and that he was passable with a staff. She told him a bow generally would not be much use in the type of fighting they would likely encounter on the road. In any case, they did not have any with them for him to use.

Introductions done, Boss had them all get ready to roll out. Seamus hugged Goodwin and thanked her for taking such good care of him and Ali. She shushed him and told him to, 'Get away before I get too mushy'. He shook the blacksmith's hand then climbed up on his wagon ready to go.

Boss' cart took the lead with Seamus and Tom in the centre. The blacksmith's apprentice was returning home to Duncameron for a visit while his foot healed. Megan took the rear position. Abel rode at the front checking the route as he was working as a guard on this journey. He would take turns with the other guards riding the front and rear.

Seamus could not actually say much about the first day of travel. He could not describe the scenery, and he and Tom did not talk much except for Tom to pass on instructions. All his attention was taken up with keeping his team moving and making sure they did not leave the road, or run into the cart in front, or go so slow they were in danger of being run into from the cart behind. He was so relieved when they finally stopped for the evening.

Tom talked him through uncoupling the horses from the wagon and tying them to a lead line for the night. He helped Seamus brush, feed, and water them. Before settling down for their evening meal he and Tom put up their sleeping quarters, a tent that attached to the side of the cart. Their work done, they joined the others by the fire.

He managed to get through the meal, just, but was so weary he almost fell asleep sitting up. Tom finally told him to go to bed. 'The guards will take turns on watch, we should only have to take a turn if one of them falls sick. So make sure you get a good nights sleep. Goodnight.' Seamus left him to join the others by the fire.

'Goodnight.' Seamus yawned as he crawled into his bedroll and was soon fast asleep. The next thing he knew Megan was shaking him awake.

'It's sun-up sleepyhead.' She laughed at him. 'Come on, we have to take the tent down before breakfast as Dad likes to get moving pretty sharply.'

Seamus stumbled around trying to help Megan with the tent until she shooed him away. Able came over to help her stow it and their bedrolls in the trunk attached to the back of the cart. He went to see the horses were fed and watered and ready to continue their journey.

Once they were on their way the second day was pretty much the same as the first, with the exception that they passed through a couple of small villages. Seamus found he could not go straight to bed after dinner that night as it was his turn to help with washing the dishes. It seemed everyone took their turn at the camp jobs. As he started to doze, his thoughts drifted to Aliah, wondering if she was all right. He was still very annoyed with her, but he meant her no ill. She should have been at Port Isby, probably even on a ship heading for home. He hoped she was closer to her goal than he was.

After two days of constant movement Aliah appreciated the stillness of the night as she sat squashed between two crates of goods slowly nibbling some bread and cheese. Pulling her cloak around her to settle down to sleep in her cramped space she dreamed longingly of the bed at Healer Goodwin's, probably exaggerating how soft it had been. But she was warm, she had food in her stomach, and the healer's medicine meant she was on the mend.

It could have been worse, much worse in fact. She had

found soon after starting her journey that the cost of travel was high, so she had to do some ducking and diving to get to where she was. She was lucky she had not had to go back to the healer's place and swallow her pride.

As Aliah started to doze, she guiltily wondered where Seamus was. She had kicked herself a number of times for not thinking to leave him a note in his pack to let him know what she was planning, and for him not to worry about her. That had always been her downfall, acting before totally thinking things through. On reflection, if she had spoken to Seamus he might have agreed with her plan and she would have had some company and maybe even been able to sleep in a bed.

Instead, she had repaid his kindness by running out on him without a word. Her only consolation was that she was putting Aria first. She vowed when she got home, she would contact the Wizards on the Isle and make sure he was going to be fine when he arrived. She owed him that at least. And she would send a note of thanks to Healer Goodwin when this was all over, explaining why she had to leave so suddenly. She was sure the healer would understand that matters of state came before any other considerations. She would send her a thank you gift just to be sure though. But before all of that she had to get home.

Day three was to be their last full day on the road before reaching Duncameron. Seamus had expected it to be as uneventful as the other two days, but he was in for a surprise. At midday they stopped by a river to rest the horses and have something to eat.

Not long after they had pulled off the road a group of five riders galloped past heading towards Sunnydale. They had begun to see more people on the road as they drew closer to the larger town, so Seamus did not think this was anything unusual. That was until the guards ordered them to move their wagons into a triangle. Tom was asked to stay out of sight in the middle of the wagons, and the rest prepared to fight.

It was then Seamus noticed the dust coming back along the road as the five riders returned, escorting a sixth man dressed in black with a wizard's lightening bolt sigil clearly showing on his chest. It was coloured silver, showing he had nearly reached the top rank of wizards. There was no doubt they were heading straight for the group of carts and, by the look on their faces, their purpose was not friendly.

Boss stepped out to meet them, with Abel at his shoulder. Abel had his sword drawn, and Boss had his hand on the hilt of his.

'Whoa,' said Boss commandingly. 'Slow down! You will have our horses bolting, rushing by at that pace.'

'We do not,"rush by",' the wizard responded in an imperious tone. 'I have sensed one of your party is a person we are looking for. You will hand them over to us!'

'We don't want any trouble,' Boss answered. 'But all of our party are well known to me and I cannot for the life of me think why one of the king's wizards would be looking for any of them. Perhaps you could explain who it is you are looking for and why, and perhaps we can let

BEGINNINGS

you know if that person is amongst us.' Grunt and Helen moved up to stand on either side of Boss, hands on the hilts of their swords, signalling they would let their visitors no closer without an explanation. Seamus stayed back by the wagons with Megan.

The wizard visibly sighed, as if this was some troublesome intervention he did not need. 'You will introduce me to all your team and I will decide if they are who I am looking for.'

Megan moved closer to Seamus. 'Helen says you are good with knives?' she whispered.

Seamus nodded, without taking his eyes off the wizard and his men.

'Good enough to just miss someone?'

Seamus nodded.

'Ok, you take the two on the left, and I will take the three on the right. As soon as anyone moves forward or goes to get off their horse, you throw a knife in front of them as a warning. Yes?'

Seamus nodded once more, still not taking his eyes off the men in front of them.

'Well, I guess we will not be doing that,' Boss said. 'Although you wear the king's robes your men do not wear royal colours. So I am thinking you might be on the king's business, but it is just as likely you are not. And even if you were, you have no right to question honest folk without a warrant, and as you have not produced one, I am thinking you do not have one. So, with respect, I think you should be on your way and leave honest folk to get on with their work.'

The wizard looked directly at a man on his right, who

started to get off his horse. Seamus resisted the urge to make the horse move as he was sure someone had told him once wizards could sense other wizards using magic. Besides he had never tried using it on an animal before. As the man's foot hit the ground one of his knives landed about a hand-span in front of it. The man halted where he stood, looking at the wizard for further instructions.

'As I said, I think you had best be on your way,' Boss told them, without even flinching. 'The next one will wound, the third will maim, and the fourth ...'

'You dare to challenge me? I am on the king's business,' the Wizard said through gritted teeth. 'And I sense the one I look for is here. You would do well to let me search.'

'And you would be best to have a warrant!' Boss did not waver.

An odd sensation like the wind rustling in his head caused Seamus to frown as the wizard's face took on a glazed expression.

'He is consulting with someone,' Megan whispered.

Seamus shook his head, unused to feeling magic being worked around him, and surprised Megan could feel what the Wizard was doing. He looked at her, shock clearly written on his face.

She merely met his gaze. 'I have a little skill, enough to know when magic is around, something you and I might talk about later.' They all held still until the wizard's gaze focused again on Boss.

'Very well. Johnson, you are to ride ahead to Duncameron. Talk to the magistrate, my mentor, one of the highest ranked Wizard of Gold, is arranging a warrant. You will bring it back to me. The rest of you, we will follow this

BEGINNINGS

group to make sure no one leaves.' The man on the ground remounted as one of their number took off for Duncameron.

Boss and Abel walked back to the carts, picking up Seamus' knife on the way. Helen and Grunt stayed between the wizard and their group, faces impassive, hands on their sword hilts. The four on the outside of the triangle watered the horses and passed about food. Boss whispered to Tom to stay under the cover of their wagon and try not to be seen. He did not want their *guests* to know they had an additional person who could not fight, as he could be targeted should things turn nasty.

Able took three horses to where Grunt and Helen stood, and the three guards mounted. Once they were in their saddles, Megan, Seamus, and Boss took their seats and moved the carts onto the road. Megan in front this time, Seamus in the middle, and Boss behind.

'We ride all the way through to Duncameron,' Boss ordered as they started moving.

They kept a steady pace throughout the afternoon. Every now and then the rustling sound disturbed Seamus, letting him know magic was being worked. A couple of times he turned around to see what the wizard was doing, and each time he caught the wizard looking at him curiously. It was a tense journey. At any moment he expected to see the rider return with the warrant.

As the sun continued its path through the sky, Seamus concentrated on keeping his team at a steady pace, and when he looked up he was surprised to see the wizard steering his horse towards his wagon.

'You, there?'

Seamus wearily watched the wizard come closer.

'Yes. You, boy. I can feel some magic in you. How about you help me find who I am looking for and I will offer you something someone of your station could never hope for: a place to train at the Wizard Isles.'

Until that precise moment it was what Seamus thought he wanted. As he looked into the cruel, hard eyes of the man riding beside him, he knew he did not want to be like this man, full of his own sense of entitlement. He had been brought up to serve the people of Hand and the Southern Duchy, and he had believed the wizards from the Isle were there to serve as well. But this man seemed to think his position put him above the law.

Without any intention of helping him, Seamus asked, 'Who is it you look for?'

The wizard's face curled into a snarl. 'An ungrateful wench. A blonde-haired, blue-eyed girl about your age who has decided her betters do not know what is right for her. She has run away from her betrothed and needs to be brought to heel.'

Seamus hoped the look he gave the wizard was one of wide-eyed astonishment. Inside he was sincerely pleased that Aliah was far away from this man. 'What makes you think she is with us? None of the women here meet that description.'

'I can smell her.'

The way the wizard said it made Seamus' stomach heave.

'If she is not here, then one of you has been near her in the last few days.'

'And why would a wizard be interested in a girl running from her wedding?' Helen pulled her horse up in between Seamus and the wizard.

BEGINNINGS

'Because she is the king's daughter,' he snarled at her. 'She is to marry a king and cement our two nations. Such a great honour, but the ungrateful girl does not know what is good for her.'

'I cannot think why anyone would refuse the match when you put it in terms like that.'

Helen's irony was clearly lost on the wizard when he said, 'Exactly'.

'We think she has been travelling with a boy, an untrained magic user. Some foolish people are hailing them as the wizard and warrior from the old tales because she carries a sword. But do not let that romantic claptrap fool you. They are both very dangerous.'

'I am sure they are.' Helen raised an eyebrow that only Seamus could see, and he chuckled into his chest. 'Now, away with you. This boy is supposed to be concentrating on his job.'

'Don't forget my offer boy,' the Wizard said as he pulled at the reins and kicked his horse, then headed back to his own party.

'What did he mean, Helen, about boys like me not being allowed into the Wizard Isle to train?' Seamus asked before Helen rode off to keep an eye on the wizard.

'Megan sensed last night that you are leaking out magic, something untrained wizards do. She is a magic finder. In the past, parents would send boys like you to the Wizard Isles. But the last year or so many boys who are not of the "right heritage" have failed to gain entry. It seems people with no money for fees are no longer accepted on the Isle. This has many people grumbling.'

'How is that he has not sensed Megan's magic?' Seamus

wondered out loud.

'She is a woman, and women with magic do not count as true magic users to those of his kind.' Helen answered disdainfully as she rode off to join Grunt at the back of the wagons.

'You have magic? How awesome.'

Seamus had forgotten that Tom was hiding in the wagon behind him until the other boy spoke. 'Just a little,' Seamus answered. 'Not even enough to light a flame.'

'Still ...' Tom's voice came from behind. Then, changing the subject he said, 'Funny that the princess ran away from her intended, and your sister did too. And they are both blonde with blue eyes.' If it were not for Tom's open and honest nature, Seamus would have believed he had actually put two and two together and come up with the truth.

'Maybe it is a sign people should stop arranging marriages for girls to suit their own ends, and let the girls choose,' Seamus responded.

'I agree,' Tom said. 'I am going to see my Maisie tomorrow, and I would not like it one bit if her father told her who to marry, even if it were me. Because I know Maisie would do the opposite just to spite him.' Tom then spent the next few candle-marks extolling the virtues of his fair Maisie.

As the afternoon rolled on to night, the pace slowed as both horses and their humans were getting weary. Just when he thought he would fall asleep at the reigns, Seamus swore he could see lights twinkling in the distance, and he sighed with relief. Still, it was another good candle length before they would come to the outskirts of Duncameron. Seamus was startled from his stupor by a voice close by.

'I know it is you, boy. You have been with the princess. I can smell it on you.'

Seamus could not see the wizard, but he could feel the waves of darkness rolling off him and his stomach churned in response.

'Tell me where she is,' he hissed.

Controlling his voice, he projected a calmness he did not feel. 'I really do not know what you are talking about. I have enough worries of my own without any trouble from you. Please, leave me alone.'

'You heard the boy.' Abel's voice came from the darkness. 'Leave him alone.'

Snorting his anger, the wizard turned his horse and headed towards the back of the caravan.

'You have really made a friend there.' Tom laughed from behind him.

'I don't wish to anger a wizard,' Seamus said. 'But I really have no idea what he is on about.' Although he said the words out loud, Seamus was sick to the stomach. How could the wizard know he had been with Aliah? Could he really smell her on him? And if he could, how was he going to get away from him?

When they finally reached Duncameron the gates to the main town were closed for the night. Megan led them through the streets that had spilled out from the old town to an inn with a large stable yard nestled in the shelter of the walls. Boss expertly backed the carts into the inn's courtyard. Seamus and Boss untethered the horses and took them into the stables to feed and tend them, while Megan went to speak with the innkeeper.

Under cover of moving the horses, Seamus smuggled Tom into the stables. Two of the wizard's men moved to the door to make sure no one left without their knowing. Helen and Grunt went and stood behind them to ensure they left the others alone to get on with their work.

'Right,' Boss whispered, as he bought a horse into the stall where Seamus was settling his horses in for the night. 'It is pretty clear for some reason the wizard wants you.' Seamus went to argue, but Boss held up his hand. 'I really do not want to know, because what I don't know, I can't tell. I know these men do not have a warrant for you, and lately there have been too many good men taken by wizards and their friends not to be seen again. I do not want to see that happen to you. So here's the plan.'

'Megan is arranging with the innkeeper to smuggle you out through the back and take you to a friend of mine. He will be able to help you control the magic Megan says is leaking out of you. He can also deal with the smell the wizard sniffer has found. Here is your pay.' He handed Seamus the three coins he was due. 'Now go wait at the back of the stables and be ready to go.'

'Thank you,' Seamus said. 'But won't you get into trouble when they find out I have left?'

'Well, doing the right thing can always get you in trouble, but I don't think they will notice for a bit. And if they do, I have a feeling we are better off saying you escaped than them finding you with us and confirming their suspicions. I plan to have Tom bed down in here to look after the horses, so they will likely assume he is you, unless they get a look at him walking, and we can prevent that for a little while.'

BEGINNINGS

'Are you sure? What about the wizard saying he could smell me?' Seamus asked.

'Megan can work a small magic, make a distracting smell for a bit. Now grab your things and go wait in the back corner over there. Helen or someone will show you the way out.'

'Thank you,' Seamus said. 'For the work and the help.'

Boss looked abashed and mumbled, 'It's all right,' before turning back to the horse Seamus had been tending to finish his work. Seamus went over to the pile of bags that had been unloaded from the carts and grabbed his possessions.

He had not been there long when a head appeared at his feet.

'Oi,' the boy whispered. 'You are to follow me. Be quiet now as they have lookouts posted around the yard.' He then proceeded to push aside a couple of boards to make a hole big enough for Seamus to crawl through.

Once outside, they crouched down, and crawled along a narrow path between stacked barrels until they hit a fence. The boy pushed open a small gate and, crouching low, Seamus followed him through it. The boy reached back and re-fastened the gate.

'Shh.' He motioned with his fingers to his lips. 'This way and be fast! Old Earl at the gate will not hold it open for long. Stick to the shadows behind me and we will not be seen unless someone is truly looking for anyone trying to escape.'

Seamus struggled to keep up with the nimble young boy, weary as he was from a long day of travelling. They soon made it to the small gate beside the main gate into

Duncameron.

'Slip him a coin.' The lad motioned to the guard standing by the partially open gate. As Seamus reached into his purse, the sound of running feet drifted from some distance behind him. 'Quick as you can,' the boy said. 'I think we may have been spotted. Better make it two coins, Earl will need to delay whoever is behind us.'

Seamus gave two of his small supply of coins to the gatekeeper, who ushered them through the opening and firmly shut the gate behind them.

'This way.' The boy motioned, and Seamus followed him through the maze of streets, completely reliant on the slippery figure as he moved further and further into the darkness of the town. They wove their way in and out of alleyways and streets until the boy finally stopped outside a door. Weary to the core, Seamus nearly stumbled over the boy as he stopped, but caught himself just in time.

Knocking twice, he paused, then knocked twice again. A few short moments later the door opened a crack, a head looked out, then up and down the street. An elderly looking man opened the door, and motioned them in. The boy handed the man a letter, which he immediately read.

'I had best get back, quick smart,' the boy said. 'Two coins is customary for guiding.'

'You young scallywag,' the elderly man said as he chuckled. 'It is only one if you are not stopped.'

'We was nearly stopped.' He looked hopefully at Seamus. 'Awright, one then.' He held out his hand and Seamus reached into his purse again and gave the last of his driving coins to his guide.

'Thank you,' he said as the boy took off.

BEGINNINGS

'Well, don't dilly-dally in the street, else all our good work will be undone,' his host advised, and Seamus blindly followed him into the hallway of the darkened house, then into the front room.

It was a small, neat front room, sparsely furnished, but snug looking with tightly drawn curtains. There were books over every surface, and the small plate of food on the arm of a chair showed the man's evening meal had been interrupted by Seamus' arrival. The man peeked through the closed curtains to check the street, then he pulled his head back into the room, frowned at Seamus, and advised him to follow if he wanted to stay safe. Seamus trailed after him into the hallway, and through the door he opened.

'Down there.' He motioned. 'And be quick!'

'But it's a cellar,' Seamus said in a shocked voice.

'I know. But it is best you be there than here for the moment. Haven't time to explain.' And then he showed he was not as old and feeble as he appeared by pushing Seamus through the door and shutting it firmly behind him.

Exhausted, stunned and scared out of his wits, Seamus had reached a point where he simply did not know what to do next. Should he bang on the door and demand to be let out? Or should he go quietly down the stairs and wait? If he did the first he risked being found by his pursuers, if he did the second there was a chance he had just been kidnapped and would be aiding his assailants. So he stood there, undecided.

'I got this far,' he said to himself. 'Only to be locked in a cellar.' His face twisted into a smile. He could stand here all night, but he really needed to eat and sleep, so he may as well find himself somewhere more comfortable. He stumbled down the stairs in the dark then proceeded to set up his sleeping gear, which, fortunately, was on the top of his pack. When he was comfortable he rummaged around and found some dried fruit and travel bread. With his hunger quietened, it did not take long before the day caught up with him and he was sound asleep.

Travelling in her cramped hiding space was uncomfortable, and it was boring. She had nothing to do for hours on end, and she could not even really hear the conversations of the people around her. At best she could hear muffled voices, at worst there was just the creaking and moving of the cargo around her. Perhaps the only good thing about it was that she was resting a lot and her strength was coming back to her. That and the fact Healer Goodwin's medicine made her sleep often.

The third day of travel was the worst though. The first two days had been relatively short, and by limiting her water intake she had been able to manage by sneaking out at night to take care of nature. But the third day for some reason was much longer. They did not stop until well into the night, and Aliah was bursting. A quick peak out of her hiding place showed her that there were too many people around for her to risk getting out.

She stifled a groan as she sat back down, wondering how long before her companions went to bed and she could sneak out? Then she realised that this was not like the other nights. There was no sound of camp being set up, and the horse hooves sounded like they were on cobblestones, not dirt.

Had they come to the end of the journey already? Aliah's mind began churning over. Would they unload tonight? If they did, would she be able to escape? And how far would she be able to run with an achingly full bladder?

Taking a deep breath she slowed her breathing the way her father's sword master had shown her when he taught her to fight. As she concentrated on her breathing she did not notice someone start to undo the canvas on the other side of her hiding place, she nearly jumped out of her skin when a voice came out of the darkness beside her.

'Crawl quietly towards me. Try not to make a noise or disturb anything. When you get to the side, slide out your bag. I will catch it. Then roll yourself out and follow me. Don't try to run away, you will be caught.'

A number of choice words her father would not approve of her uttering ran through her head. How had he known she was here? Did he mean her harm? Was there any way she could get out without following his directions?

'Quickly now. There is a king's wizard here. I suspect he is looking for you. He will find you easily enough if you don't follow my directions. And I am assuming you do not want that to happen.'

A wizard? Here? How did that happen? How could she not notice that? Should she trust this person, or should she give herself over to the wizard? Then she remembered her father's chief advisor, the wizard, Millard, and the way he looked as she boarded the ship when she left home. He was gleeful, almost as if he somehow gained something from her departure. She did not trust him.

Her mind was made up. Slowly getting the circulation back into her limbs she began to move.

'Hurry up,' her rescuer whispered.

'I am going as fast as I can,' she whispered back. 'I would like to see you move fast after having been cramped like this all day,' she almost said, but bit her tongue. She managed to slide her bag and her cloak-wrapped sword through the hole.

'*Wait.*' Footsteps moved away from the canvas, there was some mumbling, then someone was back. 'Now it is your turn. Quietly, though. That wizard and his friends are a suspicious lot.'

Aliah began to slide her body round the crates she had been squashed between all day. It was not as easy as it seemed, and her skirt caught between two crates and the whole load began to topple.

'Hey, what's going on there?' someone shouted.

'It is just me,' the voice beside her said. 'I was trying to get my gear out for tonight, was not paying attention and just about brought some crates down.'

'Well, be more careful. Any breakages come out of your wages.'

'I will." He dropped his voice to a whisper. "And so will you.'

She had frozen during the exchange, but now worked her skirt free and made it to the opening in the canvas. With all her might she tried to roll herself over the side, but after her illness and sitting for three days, she was just not strong enough.

'Here. Let me help.' A strong arm snaked through the gap, grabbed her round the waist and rolled her up the side of the wagon, through the gap, then down the other side. The world looked topsy-turvy for a moment, then she was upright staring directly at a man who she guessed to be about five and twenty. He was carrying quite a number of knives, and there was as sword at his side. He looked her up and down. 'Can you walk?'

She nodded back at him. 'So long as it is not far.'

'Oh, it is not far at all. Boss wants a word with you.'

Aliah's stomach clenched, and she almost lost control of her bladder there and then. He grabbed her arm, picked up her gear, and pulled her to the front of the two wagons.

'Good, let's go while all their attention is on the barn.' He pulled her towards the back of the building.

'*Hey.*'

Instead of stopping, the man pulled her faster in behind the building, then popped his head around into the yard to see what was happening.

'Whew. Looks like they were calling someone else. In here.' He pushed her roughly through a door, which let to a hallway. On one side she could hear the hustle and bustle of a kitchen, the door on the other side was closed. He opened that door and pushed her through. 'Wait here.'

Before he could shut the door Aliah put her foot in it. 'My possessions?' she asked.

He flashed a smile, and she imagined she could see real humour in his eyes. 'Good try, but I know the feel of a sword.'

Aliah shrugged, it was worth a try. 'How about a trip to the privy before you lock me up? I have not been since last night.'

Was that genuine sympathy in his eyes? 'Sorry, cannot

let you back out there. Too dangerous. For you and for us. I will get one of the girls to bring you a chamber pot.'

He locked the door behind him but, true to his word, he opened it for a girl a few moments later. A pot was passed through. He did not close the door, but he and the girl gave her privacy so she could take care of herself. Once the pot was removed the door was again closed and Aliah was left alone in the dark.

10
NIGHTS IN A CELLAR

Seamus awoke as sunlight streamed down the stairs to the cellar. He blinked in the stark light as his eyes adjusted to the room, then groggily got to his feet. The morning light revealed two beds against the walls of the cellar, and he cursed himself for his stupidity at not lighting a match the night before. At the very least he could have slept in comfort.

'Apologies to you, I did not mean for you to stay here so long last night. There were patrols out on the street in larger numbers than normal all night, and there were definitely wizards with them.' The elderly man looked even older in the bright sunlight, after a sleepless night. 'I have coffee on the stove and breakfast cooking. No need to bring your bags up, we can sort them out later.'

Seamus stumbled up the stairs and followed his host into a room at the back of the house which, given the smells coming from there, was the kitchen.

'Please, sit down.' The man gestured to the table that was positioned in the middle of the room. When he was seated the man proceeded to dish up two plates loaded with bacon and mushrooms and tomatoes. Seamus immediately began devouring his as if he had not seen a meal in weeks, stopping only to drink some of the cool water that was already on the table. His host placed down cups of milky, steaming coffee, and then joined him at the table. He was about halfway through his meal when he placed down his knife and fork and looked at Seamus.

'That was a big ruckus last night and, if it was all to find you, someone wants you pretty badly. If that is the case then you are way more important than Boss Allum realised. He asked me to take care of you, to teach you how to shield your magic, and then get you home to your family. Before I commit to helping you, I need to make sure you are who you say you are, and that by helping you I will not be putting myself or others at risk

'I am going to finish my meal, and then I am going to tell you a bit about me. I do not do this lightly as even knowing a little bit about me may get you into trouble and compromise my security. I would appreciate it if you would give me enough of your story to let me know whether I should help you or not, and what I might actually be able to do to help you. If you choose not to tell me the truth—and believe me after you hear my story you will know I have the resources to tell whether or not you do—then I am happy for you to leave.' He looked steadily at Seamus, and then carried on eating.

Seamus kept his head down, no longer enjoying his food. The man knew there was more to his story than he had told Boss. He would help, but the cost was to tell him the truth. How much of the truth would he actually be able to share without compromising his family or Aliah? How much should he tell given the wizard from yesterday was clearly not going to give up searching for him? Finally, after what seemed an age, his host finished his last mouthful and refilled both their coffees.

'I am of a mind to start now, but you feel free to keep eating.' He smiled, but the smile did not really touch his eyes.

Seamus placed his knife and fork down on his plate and stared at the elderly man. Looking at him in this light, he did not seem quite as old as he had last night. His light blue eyes were clear, if a little weary from a night without sleep. His greying hair was a little unkempt, but there was still plenty of brown through it. The wrinkles Seamus remembered seeing on his face last night were no longer there. In fact, if he did not know better, the man might only be ten or so years older than his father.

'I will not be starting with my name, that you will have when I know the truth of you. This is to protect both of us, as knowing who I am could put you in danger. And if you tell the wrong people you know me, well, that would place me in serious danger as well. For the moment you can call me Walter, as many do, and I will continue to call you Sean. So we will start with what happened last night.'

'It seems a silver wizard was very interested in finding you so Boss Allum had you brought to me. Where you stayed last night, although not comfortable, was a warded room. That means only a very strong wizard would have been able to find you. A large number of people were searching for you for most of the night. They have stopped for the moment, possibly to regroup, so we have a small opportunity to decide our next step.' He paused to drink some of his coffee, and Seamus followed his every move.

'You want to know how I know they have stopped?' He looked at a surprised Seamus. 'I can feel they have stopped using magic to sense you, just as I can sense you through your magic. As an untrained wizard you are leaking magic almost continuously. This broadcasting will only get stronger unless you learn the most basic of techniques to control it.'

'And the only way you would know that is if you were a wizard yourself,' Seamus interrupted. 'And that would mean you are working for the same people as those who are following me.' Seamus moved as if to get up and leave.

'Settle down.' Walter calmly carried on drinking his coffee. 'While all those who call themselves wizards do report to the grand wizard, I do not call myself wizard and have not done so for a few years. In fact, there are many of us who no longer use the title, but that does not mean we are not strong in magic.

'There are many magic users out there from herb women to water diviners who use magic but are not wizards. It is true that men strong in magic are to be trained and regulated by the wizard council on the Wizard Isles, and for a while I was. In fact, I was a teacher of trainee wizards before I left.

'However, I became aware of some corruption and strange goings on there, and when I tried to investigate I was demoted from my position. I became a village healer and then, when I could no longer trust the actions of my fellow wizards, I left the order all together.

'After I left my post I wandered until I came into contact with a group of people who had heard of my issues with the wizards' council and knew of their corruption. Apparently it had been building for years. These people are allied with some other magic users, I am not at liberty to tell you anything about who these people are as it could place them in danger. What I can say is that we have been gathering information and watching events, waiting for our chance to thwart their grand scheme. The wizard who looked for you last night is known to be loyal to one of the inner-circle of plotters. Because of this, I was asked to look after you and get you away because we do not trust their intentions.

'Boss thought the Wizard was looking for you because your magic is very strong. I have to say I personally think it very unlikely that all those soldiers last night would have been mobilised for a mere magic user, no matter how potentially powerful a wizard they would make.'

'Is there not a danger that uncontrolled magic can be harmful?' Seamus asked, feeling a little sheepish because he knew so very little on the subject.

Walter laughed. 'That is a common myth. It has been

rumoured that in the past people who could not control their magic have exploded, killing themselves and others around them. I have never seen this happen, in fact my experience leads me to believe that the body can only take in as much magic as it can safely hold, and it gets rid of anything it cannot cope with, hence the leaking of magic in untrained mages.'

'Oh,' Seamus tried not to feel foolish. 'So Boss and his crew are part of the group you talked about?'

'I really should not say anything more about them,' Walter responded. 'At least not until I know your story. I have told you much about myself, I hope you guard my secret as carefully as you guard your own.

Seamus gnawed on his lip while he considered how much he should tell Walter about himself and about Aliah. Decision made, he took a deep breath and began.

'Up until Sunnydale I had been travelling with a girl. We told people she was my sister, but she was not. We were heading in the same direction and it suited us to travel together. We parted ways at Sunnydale. It seems the wizard last night could smell that I had been with her, and that is why he is looking for me.'

Walter raised his eyebrows and indicated that Seamus should continue.

'Her story is not mine to tell, and I will not betray her secrets. I will just say that what she was doing was important for all of Aria, and she was brave to be doing it, if a little foolish in her approach.'

Seamus could not be sure, but it looked like Walter was holding back a chuckle. 'And you, young man, what is your story?'

BEGINNINGS

'I left home because I realised I had magic and I needed someone to teach me how to control and use it. I had thought to go to the Wizard Isle and ask to be trained there. Now I am not so sure. I did not like that wizard on the road. He really gave me the creeps and he seemed to be saying that a common boy would not be accepted there, but if I gave up my friend then he would make an exception.'

Walter agreed. 'Yes, it appears things have changed since I left. Now only the sons of the well to do who can pay fees are accepted. Listening to you though, I would be surprised if your parents were not wealthy enough to be able to pay the fees the school sets.'

Seamus ignored the lead to give him more information. 'Then one of Boss' crew seemed to be saying that the wizards were responsible for the disappearance of certain people. That also made me uncomfortable.'

'It is true the wizards no longer have the confidence of many people, and that number becomes greater the closer you get to Bannock. So you will return home now and find someone close to home to train you?'

Seamus could feel himself going red under Walter's scrutiny. How much should he tell the man? He gnawed on his lip again. Walter had been a teacher of wizards, maybe if he told him everything he would take Seamus on as a kind of apprentice?

'I cannot do that.' Seamus admitted. 'Where I come from magic is not permitted. Now they know I have it I can never return home.'

Walter raised his eyebrows in surprise. 'You are from Hand? No ... wait ... you are. And if I remember rightly only the ruling family has magic running through it. So you are the duke's son? By your age ... You must be his oldest son. Well, I'll be ...'

It appeared Walter was speechless, so Seamus continued. 'I am Seamus, and I was heir to the Duchy before all this happened. I cannot go home and I need a teacher. I was hoping that maybe ...

Walter suddenly found his voice again. 'Oh, no. Not me. Not in a million years. I am satisfied with what I have here, and I would be hard pressed to explain you away. No, do not look at me like that. It would be too dangerous for both of us if you stayed, especially since the wizards already know you are here in Duncameron. I can alter how I appear to others so I can hide in plain sight, but I could not do that for both of us.' As if he could not bear to look at Seamus' crestfallen face he immediately began clearing the dishes.

'I can teach you to manage your leaking and how to only draw magic when your stores are low. That I will do for you, because if I do not, then you will surely be caught. But that is all I can do.'

Seamus did not know what to say. He helped Walter with the dishes in silence. His gut was churning. He did not want to go to train with the wizards on their island. He could not stay here because Walter was right, it was too dangerous to do so. What should he do? As his thoughts wandered through his options, a rustling brushed his head.

'Quick. Seamus, take that food and water from the bench and head to the basement. Quickly now! I feel the magic stirring.' Walter grabbed a candlestick holder and some candles and followed Seamus.

BEGINNINGS

Feeling an odd prickling at the back of his neck, Seamus looked at Walter, who looked closely at him. 'You can feel it too, I see. We have not got much time.'

As they entered the basement Walter pulled the door closed behind him. Seamus noticed there was a handle on the inside, and laughed at how worried he had been last night about being locked in. He was soon settled in, and more comfortably than the night before now he could use a bed.

'Right,' Walter said. 'I have a plan of sorts, well for today at least. I need to go and talk with some friends of mine. We will need their support to leave Duncameron. In the meantime I need you to stay here in the basement. I know it is not great, but you cannot be detected here unless they send some stronger wizards from the Isle, which would take time.'

'How long will you be?' Seamus asked, not happy about spending any more time in the basement.

'As short a time as I need, but by supper time at the latest. That would be about two candles time. If I am not back by then you will need to assume something has happened to me. If I can, I will try and send someone to find you if it looks likely there will be any trouble.'

Walter looked Seamus straight in the eye. 'At the moment you are a big liability. A blood sensor, such as the one you met yesterday needs to be within sight of a person to get a full reading, but you are broadcasting your magical ability far and wide. While I am gone, I need you to practice shielding your magic.'

Seamus frowned. 'I don't know what you mean.'

'I know, but you need to trust me on this. I have taught

many a young wizard to shield and control their talent. Admittedly, it can take weeks, but I need you to learn quicker than that. This will tire you, but you need to keep practicing all day for me.'

Seamus nodded. 'All right.' He settled and Walter asked him to closed his eyes and breathe deeply in and out, and relax his muscles. It was so much like the concentration techniques used before weapons practice that Seamus found it easy to follow.

'Now you are relaxed, I need you to keep your eyes closed and concentrate on your body. Can you feel around your heart a pulsating warmth?'

Seamus focussed. He felt the warmth, and as soon as he felt it he lost it in his excitement. He went through the relaxation techniques again, and after his third attempt, he managed to feel the pulse without losing it.

'Good,' Walter praised. 'Now I need you to concentrate on that warm pulse and push it to the ends of your fingers. You need to imagine it moving from your centre through your chest and down your arms until it reaches the end of your fingers.'

Seamus concentrated but could not move the pulse. He broke out in a sweat as he lost the pulse again.

'No one does it the first time,' Walter assured him. 'Do not think of the pulse as being separate from you, think of it as your lifeblood, and that it has channels to move along to the end of your fingers.'

Seamus began again. At first he managed to move the pulse to his arms, but was so surprised he lost his hold. He kept trying until he finally managed to get the pulse to his fingers. He could hear from Walter's voice

BEGINNINGS

that he was pleased with his progress.

'Now slowly bring the pulse back to the centre.' This process also took a number of tries before Seamus could send the pulse down to his fingers and back to the centre. When he achieved it he opened his eyes to find Walter smiling.

'Good. Very good. I am sure you have already found that you can move objects by willing it if you concentrate hard enough. Maybe even sometimes without meaning to. When doing this you have been using the magic that pulses inside of you. When you try to move an object you are pushing it out. What you have just learnt is the first step in beginning to control the magic, or the pulse. Now eat something then I will show you how to shield your pulse from others.'

Seamus was surprised to find he actually needed to eat, even though it was only a candle-mark since breakfast.

'Magic uses energy, as much as physical exercise does. If you have not used it for a while you will burn more energy, much like if you are unfit and you do physical activity,' Walter explained as Seamus ate some bread spread with a soft cheese. When he finished Walter restarted the lesson.

'Find your pulse again, push it to your fingers, bring it back to the centre. Good. Now in your mind make the pulse as small as you can, until you barely feel it.'

Seamus concentrated then looked up when he felt he could make the pulse no smaller. 'That is good,' said Walter. 'Already your broadcast is quieter. Now we have to hide it so no one can hear it.'

Seamus opened his eyes. 'Hide it? How?'

Walter patiently told him. 'Repeat the exercise.' He waited until Seamus confirmed he had done it, and he himself could feel the magical vibration quieten. 'Now, I need you to imagine that small pulse as a hard object, and I need you to imagine putting that object in a box and closing it.'

Seamus felt Walter watching him as he tried to hide his magic. Just when he thought he had it hidden, Walter's searching probe found the pulse and freed it from its bonds.

'*Goddess,*' Seamus exploded.

Walter laughed. 'No that is good! You managed to stop the vibrations, which is good for your first time. As you get stronger you will also be able to hide yourself from other lesser wizards when they probe. And that is how a teacher will test how strong your control is.'

'I think I understand.' Seamus told his teacher.

'Right, so today you need to practice these exercises, extending your pulse then hiding it, and we will work on this until you can hide your pulse without needing to feel the extension first. The step after that is to keep your power hidden until you need to use it. The final step I will teach you is to feel when your magic is low and how to draw more. Understand?'

'Yes,' Seamus mumbled, thinking it would be a slow process, given how long it had taken him to get this far.

'Fine,' Walter said. 'From the candle I can see if I do not leave soon it will be midday already. I need to meet with some friends at a tavern to find out what is happening, and await a message from some allies so we can plan. I will also ask around and find out if there are any magic users who might be prepared to take on an apprentice.

BEGINNINGS

You can keep practicing in my absence.'

With that Walter rose, climbed the stairs, and left Seamus alone. He finished eating his bread and cheese, drank some water, then continued with his exercises. While he was exercising his mind he also needed to exercise his body, but what could he do in such a confined space? An idea hit him. He started going through the main sword positions, both attack and defence, to keep his body moving.

As he did so he realised it was like a kind of dance. He wondered if one person attacked while another defended without swords, would that be a new type of fighting? Something stirred in his memories. It was not a new idea. He remembered seeing some visitors to the palace practice an unarmed combat similar to this. He wished he had someone to develop the idea further with. If only Liam was here. He stopped moving as a feeling of homesickness overwhelmed him. Sitting down on the bed he started his magic exercises again to take his mind off the loneliness he felt.

Halfway through the second candle he took another break. Half listening for the door, he tried to sleep. As soon as he heard a noise above him he jumped to his feet. The young boy from the previous night came through the basement door and stopped in his tracks, nearly dropping the bundle he had in his arms.

'I didn't mean to frighten you.' He blushed. 'Master Walter was worrying you might be fretting over his delay. Also that you might be hungry.' He tentatively came down the stairs, his blue eyes darting around from under his reddish-brown hair.

He placed the bundle gently on the floor and withdrew two covered pottery pots. Removing the lids from them he let loose a mouth watering aroma from the meat and vegetable stew and a stewed apple pudding. 'There be spoons in the bag, and another candle or two. Also some books to pass the time. I am to tell you it is not yet safe to come up, but Walter will speak with you tomorrow. If you wait a moment, I am also to bring you down some more bedding.' The boy backed away and ran up the stairs. Seamus covered his food and waited for the boy to return.

'I guess its another night underground,' he said to no one. 'I wonder why the boy seems afraid of me tonight ...'

The door above squeaked and the boy entered, burdened with a comforter and two pillows.

'It is not much.' He eyed Seamus warily. 'But it was all I could find on the beds upstairs.'

'That will do fine.' He smiled encouragingly at the boy, who blushed again. Seamus took the bedding from him and put it on one of the beds. The boy continued staring at him.

'Would you like to join me for supper?' Seamus asked. 'There is enough for two.'

The boy took a startled step back. 'Ah, uh, no thanks, I have my supper back at the tavern where I live.' He blushed again.

'Is there something you want to ask me then?' Seamus settled back on the floor beside his food. The boy looked, if anything, even more nervous. 'It is all right. I will not bite. Ask away.'

'Is it true you are a mighty wizard and have been travelling with a woman who is a fierce warrior? Like the two in the prophesy?' The words stumbled out of his mouth before he could stop them.

Seamus had to stop himself from laughing and causing the boy even more embarrassment.'Where did you hear that?' he asked.

'It be what the soldiers who are looking for you are saying. They say to keep away from the wizard and his warrior protector as you are mighty dangerous together. No approaching, just call the guards. Even if you are seen alone.'

Seamus found it harder to contain his laughter than he did to contain his magic. Finally it got the better of him and he burst out laughing. The young boy looked mortified.

'It's all right,' Seamus said to him. 'It is just that I am not much of a wizard. I have not even begun my training. And as you can see I am travelling alone. I am not sure why the soldiers are after me, but it is not for the reasons they are telling people. And if it were not for good people like you and Walter, I am not sure what would have happened to me. I really appreciate your help, and if there is anything I can do in return I will surely do it.'

The boy's face was a picture of confusion as he turned to go, then he looked back. 'I am not sure I should be telling you this, but I overheard them all talking at the tavern and I think they may have a plan for you to do something dangerous to help us. Only I am thinking if you are not a wizard, it will be a mite dangerous for you, and you might have to ask them for some other way to pay them back.' And with that, he scooted up the stairs and was gone with the click of the door behind him.

'Whatever could he mean? They have a task for me?'

Seamus took the lid off his stew and dug in. He was past hungry after the practice he had been doing that day. 'I wonder what the prophecy is that he spoke of ?'

Seamus finished his meal then had a look at the books Walter had sent. There was one on the history of the Wizard Isles, and one on the theory of magic. He read for a while, then practiced some of the sword moves again, modifying them to work better without swords.

Not wanting to spend another night in darkness, Seamus lit a new candle then lay down on his bed, tired and ready for sleep that would not come. His mind kept wandering. Where was Aliah now? Why were the wizards spreading rumours about them? To scare the public? Where would he go after Walter had taught him to control his magic? Finally his mind slowed down and he drifted off to sleep.

As with the previous morning Seamus woke to the sound of the door opening and the smell of breakfast cooking.

'It is all right to come up and eat,' Walter called down, and left the basement door open for him.

Seamus tidied up his bedding and stored his pack away, assuming he would have to return to the basement until he had his magic under control. Chores completed, he headed upstairs to the kitchen where he found Walter cooking bacon and sausages.

'You look a little worse off for your trials,' he said. 'That there is the washhouse.' He pointed to a door off to the side. 'I have heated water in a tub for you to wash, and there are some local clothes, kindly donated by some of our supporters. It would be good for us all if you cleaned up before breakfast.'

Inside the washhouse he topped up the tub with hot water and stripped off all his clothing. Washing himself and his clothes as quickly as he could, he had to admit it did feel better to clean the grime from his body. On the bench by the wall he spied clean under-garments beside a set of tight fitting trousers, and a linen over-shirt. He hung up his clothes, then dried himself on a rough piece of cloth. He put on his clean clothes before using his belt on the outside of his shirt like Walter, realising that was the only way to manage the extended length shirt. Boots back on his feet, he was finally ready to eat.

'While you are waiting you can make yourself useful.' Walter plonked a loaf of fresh bread and a crock of butter on the table as he emerged from the washhouse. Seamus took up a knife and cut the loaf into slices, and then buttered each one. He then sliced some of the cheese that was already on the table and used it to make sandwiches. He placed them on a plate ready to take downstairs.

'Well, you have made progress,' Walter stated as he continued cooking breakfast, 'Your magic is now a gentle hum, not a loud shout.'

'I do not understand how?' Seamus frowned. 'I did not consciously put up walls.'

Walter stopped what he was doing and looked at Seamus. 'The point of the exercise yesterday was to teach you how to reach your magic and how to quieten it. Your mind has done the rest. Sub-consciously your mind has worked out you will call for the magic when you need it and keeps it contained until you do.' He went back to his cooking. 'A few more days practice and only the strongest of wizards will be able to tell you have any magic at all.'

Seamus felt inordinately pleased with himself. He had been worried about how to control his magic for so long it was a relief to know he could actually do it. Deep down inside, he had also wondered if he would ever be able to learn how to use his gift in a controlled way, and he now felt more like he had a fighting chance.

They ate breakfast in silence, although Seamus was bursting to be filled in on what Walter had found out the previous day. Frustratingly, Walter continued to eat steadily and silently.

Finally he placed his knife and fork on the plate and leaned back in his chair. 'We may not have much time before they begin searching for you today. Last night we were told there will be a street-by-street search today by the soldiers. Unfortunately that means you will need to spend most of the day in the basement again. But at least it is only soldiers. They will never even see the door, let alone suspect you are down there.

'From the information we gained it seems they are looking for you and the girl you talked about together. They appear to be putting the fear of the goddess into people by telling them you are the Wizard and Warrior of Prophecy.'

Seamus had to interrupt. 'I do not think that prophecy made it to Hand, or if it did, I have never heard it.'

Walter frowned. 'That is unusual as I am pretty sure the prophecy originated in Hand or there about. Anyway, the short version is a prophecy stated in a time of extreme

BEGINNINGS

danger a wizard and warrior will appear to protect the people from a great evil.'

It was Seamus' turn to frown. 'That does not even make sense. Firstly, it tells the people there is some great danger coming, and secondly I am no wizard.'

'True, but most people will not think that way. They are just scared of the people being looked for and so will be more likely to report them. I have a sympathetic ear in the local governor's office and he has been informed they are looking for a rogue wizard and a female warrior who may know where the Princess Alihanna is. I am sure you have heard she is missing?' Walter looked rather strangely at Seamus as he said this. 'They are telling people that you are dangerous and should not be approached.'

'They do not know who I am?' Seamus asked to avoid the implied question about Aliah.

'That is what we believe,' responded Walter. 'There have been no rumours about your having left the Isle of Hand. However, that may be because of a much bigger thing on everyone's mind.'

'And that would be?'

'A merchant vessel called into Port Marden less than a six-day ago. It had passed by the Port at Ironhills in Carsten and saw a fleet of more than fifty warships loading and preparing for departure. They estimated they would be ready to sail within a short time, perhaps two or three six-days, which means they would be visible in the outer-Isles within maybe three six-days. The rumour is that this is in response to the princess refusing to marry the King of Carsten and running away. There will be a war unless the princess is found.'

Walter was silent to let the information sink in. Seamus was sure his cheeks were flushed and he was waiting for Walter to ask him a direct question about the princess. But he said nothing.

'Now you and I know, it takes more than a couple of six-days to gather that many soldiers and ships, and provision them for a sea journey of that length, while ensuring they are adequately armed. And that is how long the princess has been missing.' Walter continued when Seamus said nothing. 'To prepare a fleet for war takes many months, so this must have started before the princess even set sail. In fact we have information that tells us this was likely so.'

Seamus did not know what to say, so he said nothing. Walter was still giving him a strange look, and he was sure the man had guessed who his travelling companion had been, but he would not confirm anything out of respect for Aliah. Walter shook his head, and Seamus felt as if he had failed some sort of test.

'So, today you will practice and rest downstairs. Tonight, when it is safe, we will go down the sewers to a series of underground tunnels that lead out of the city. We have a friend that will meet on the other side of the walls, he will bring horses and will guide us through a safe passage in the mountains so we can avoid patrols. Questions?' He looked at Seamus.

'Yes. One. Where are you taking me exactly?'

'Out of Duncameron first and foremost. We will all be safer when you are gone. Our plan is to head to Bannock first. One more magic user will not be noticed there. From there we will use our network to send you to a

BEGINNINGS

teacher, either here or in Nataria.'

'Please do not think that I do not appreciate all that you and your friends have done for me, but maybe I would be better off on my own once outside of Duncameron.' Seamus did not like the feeling things were moving forward without his control. In the back of his mind he remembered what the boy said last night about him being asked to do something dangerous to help their cause.

'You can certainly do that,' Walter said to him. 'But I suggest you need to finish what I can teach you about the basics of controlling your magic before you head out alone. If you do not then you are more at risk of being caught by the wizard searching for you. It is three days ride to Bannock, and in that time you will be much more in control and can make your own decisions.'

Seamus agreed that was acceptable.

'However, I would appreciate it if you would at least come into Bannock town with me as I do need some help with an errand I have to run.'

Here we go, Seamus thought. *The scary errand the boy told me of.*

'We have something valuable we need to get into the castle and we may need someone to provide a bit of a distraction.' Walter looked keenly at him.

'Will it be dangerous?' Seamus asked.

Walter shrugged. 'Actually, we hope not to need you at all. But if we need a distraction it will just be talking to some guards to keep their attention in another direction.'

'Sounds easy,' Seamus said, skeptically.

'If all goes to plan it will be. But there is always a risk we will be caught out.'

Seamus nodded his understanding that there was potential danger. 'Can you assure me you intend no harm to anyone inside the castle?' Seamus asked.

'Most certainly not.' Walter seemed appalled at the very idea.

'All right. I will think on it.'

'That is all I can ask. Now, we should get set up downstairs as I will need to set the door ward before there are soldiers or wizards around who might feel what I am doing. Then I will sort out everything for tonight.'

For the first two candle-marks of the day Seamus concentrated on his magic techniques, then spent some time on his idea for unarmed combat. He broke for lunch and ate the sandwiches he had prepared that morning. After his midday meal he read some of the book on the history of magic and he soon felt sleepy. Aware he would be awake all night he made up his bed just after he lit the second candle and tried to get some rest.

As he started to doze, he wondered what Walter had been expecting him to say all morning. He also wondered how much he really knew about his having travelled with Aliah? Maybe he would find out on their journey to Bannock.

11
A NIGHT AT AN INN

The storeroom was dark and dank and there was nowhere to sit, which suited Aliah as she had sat down for almost the entire day. She walked around the room to loosen her muscles. Four paces across wise, six paces lengthwise. Not really enough room to walk around so she began to do some of the limbering exercises she did before weapons practice. Her body felt stiff and weak. That was what you got from illness and inactivity. She assessed it would be some time before she was up to full strength again. But at least now, she was ready to make a run for it if the opportunity arose.

She laughed to herself. What great progress she had made on her own since leaving Sunnydale. Trapped in a storeroom by strangers. She was a stow-away who could have charges brought against her. And she was only marginally closer to home. Suddenly her decision to take off on her own terms did not seem such a good one. Maybe she had been a little hasty?

Time dragged on. Still no one came for her. She sat for a while. She did some more stretches. She paced the room. She sat again. She put her ear to the door, but the corridor seemed quiet. She stood under the small window to see if she could hear anything from outside. But there was nothing. Too nervous to sleep, she sat and she paced and she sat again.

Finally the door opened and her captor entered. 'He will see you now.' He grabbed her by the arm and pulled her to her feet. He did not lose his grip on her as he marched her out of the storeroom and down the corridor to a room at the other end. She could hear the noise from the tavern through the door to her right, but he led her to the room on the left. His grip was so tight any thoughts of escape fled.

The soft lighting in the room was given from two oil lamps on the wall. The only furniture was a large square table surrounded by four sturdy wooden chairs, giving the idea this room was used for meetings.

Sitting in the chair across from the door she had entered was a large, muscle-bound man about her father's age. His face was stern as he watched her placed none to gently on the chair in front of him. Her captor went back to the door, shutting it and putting himself squarely in front of it, as if to deter any thoughts of escape.

'Now, Able, you should be a little more gentle. If that wizard is to be believed this is Princess Aliahanna. If Healer Goodwin's description is to be believed, this is Seamus' errant sister.'

'To me she is a stow-away,' the man replied from behind her. 'Anyone with an ounce of integrity pays their way in life. They do not hide away and steal.'

'I did not steal anything!' Aliah's temper flared, even though her better sense told her not to get upset.

'We in the wagon trade see stowing away as stealing. You stole space and you stole the coin we should have been paid for a lawful journey,' the man in front of her explained. To the man behind her he said, 'Able, I think this might go better if you guard the door from the other side.'

The door opened and Able grumbled under his breath as he went through. The door shut loudly behind him. Aliah was left alone with the stranger sitting in front of her. She stared at him, waiting for him to speak. He merely stared back, as if taking her measure.

Aliah could bear the silence no longer. 'What are you going to do with me? Hand me over to the authorities?'

He looked her directly in the eyes. 'That really depends on you. Or, more to the point, on what you tell me about you.'

Aliah was about to blurt out some sob story to cover her presence on the wagon, but before she could get a word out the man held up his hand. 'I do not want any lies or cover-ups. You may not realise what a dangerous situation we are in, or what we have all risked by even keeping you here.'

Aliah stopped and looked at him closely, noticing the strain around his eyes and the weariness in his posture.

'Outside the front and back doors are paid men, mercenaries. They have accompanied us most of today. They are here to see we do not leave before the wizard is satisfied we are not harbouring a runaway princess. A princess, I might add, who fits your description.

'On top of that they are now looking for a young boy who travelled with us. They say they can smell the princess on him. Yet he insists the only person he has travelled with is his sister. Strangely his sister's description also fits you.

'Normally, as a law abiding citizen, I would have handed you over to the wizard and he could work out who you are. But this wizard is with men who are not in the king's employ. And I would think the king himself would send his own men to find his daughter, not hire some mercenaries. So, I am giving you this one opportunity to tell me who you are.'

'Why not hand me over anyway if it is so much trouble?' Aliah asked somewhat defiantly.

'Because I have a daughter. And that daughter would make my life a misery if I handed a woman running away from an arranged marriage over to the authorities. She has a soft heart and strong opinions on women being treated as if they are a possessions.' A wry smile flitted across his face.

More than anything it was the last comment that decided Aliah on trusting this man. Well, at least trusting him partially. She would not land Seamus in more trouble by telling them about him. He did not deserve that after she ran out on him. But she would tell the man, who risked his life for her, everything else.

'I am Princess Aliahanna,' she told him. 'I have run away from my arranged marriage because I found out Carsten was preparing to go to war against us and they would use me as a point to rally their troops. I need to get home to my father and let him know what I have found out.'

'And I should believe you because ...?' He raised an eyebrow at her.

'There is no reason why you should believe me. And to be honest I do not really care whether you do or not. I am who I am and I have to do what I have to do regardless of what you think.' Aliah looked the man straight in the eye.

He laughed at her. 'Well, you are feisty, I will give you that. Why not just hand yourself over to the nearest garrison if you need to get back to your father?'

'Because I believe some of my father's advisors might be misleading him about the intentions of the King of Carsten. I need to speak to him before they do. That means I need to get home without being detected. So, if you will give me my things and let me go, I will be on my way.'

This time he let out a belly laugh. 'You are obviously an educated girl, I can tell by the way you speak. And you might very well be royalty. You are high handed enough for that. I have to say though, I thank the goddess that if you are the heir it will be your husband who rules, because I would not give Aria a candle-mark under your guidance.'

That was it. It was too much to take. She was tired, hungry, and a prisoner again. Then to be told she was not fit to rule her country—that was too much to bear.

'And what gives you the right to make that call? You hardly know me.'

'You know, I listen to my daughter tell me the tradition of a woman heir marrying and the crown going to her husband is outdated, and that women are capable of ruling a country. And then I think of you. I am here risking mine and my crew's lives to hide you, and you tell me to my face whether or not I believe you is not important. I am the only one at the moment who is able to get you away from those who are following you, and yet you still do not think my opinion is important. You think to walk out of here with wizards and armed men looking for you without a plan. You act on emotion, not on reasoning—'

'Father, we are not here to have a great debate on what traits a ruler should have.'

Aliah had been so engrossed in what the stranger was saying she had not realised the door opened or someone had entered.

'And as usual you have only stated half the case,' the woman continued. This girl has shown courage enough to escape her captors once before. She has demonstrated her love of country by trying to get home to warn her father of a potential war. She has shown ingenuity to get this far. She is young; patience and respect for others will come with age. I am Megan, pleased to meet you.'

Aliah smiled tentatively at the woman who had entered with a tray of food for two people. As she put the tray down, Aliah thanked her. 'But your father is right. I have this driving need to fix everything myself, and so I do sometimes act before I think. And especially before I think of others. I hope I get better at thinking through situations. I can only try.' She looked at the man in front of her. 'I am sorry, I have not even asked your name.'

'Toby Allum, but they call me Boss Allum, or Boss for short.'

'Well, Mister Allum, if I am to be entirely honest with you I do need to get home. It is urgent. I need to speak to my father, not just about the impending war, but to caution him about some of his advisors. I am tired. I am hungry and to be completely honest, I am scared. I left the one person who was helping me, thinking I could do this on my own. But the truth of the matter is I do not really believe I can. But I weigh that up against putting people in danger by asking them to help me, and I find I cannot ask them to risk their lives for me. So I must go on alone.'

'Now that is more like it.' Boss slapped his hand on the table, causing the soup in the bowl in front of him to spill over. 'Firstly, I should tell you that as a leader you often have to ask things of people that might put them at risk. A good leader is one who weighs the cost of that life before they decide.

'Secondly, I have to say I nearly believe you. Unfortunately for you though, I am not quite so easy to persuade. I have someone who can verify your story, but they will not be here until tomorrow. I believe we are safe for the moment as the search has moved to town to look for the boy.'

Aliah hoped she covered her concern for Seamus, but was doubtful as Boss Allum was sharper than he first appeared.

'Eat your food. Megan will make you a bed in the storeroom. It would be a bit obvious if we put you up in one of our rooms at the moment, especially with that wizard deciding to take rooms here to keep an eye on us. We will have to lock you in, in case anyone tries the door. But it should be all right for a night. Then we can think things through tomorrow.' Decision made, Boss Allum started eating the food on the table in front of him. Megan left them to it.

Aliah slowly ate her bread and soup, still not convinced she was not a captive. There was one way to find out. 'Boss, may I have my sword and pack back?'

Looking up at her over the rim of his bowl he searched her face, then shrugged. 'Can I have your solemn word you will not use your weapon on any of my people under any circumstances?'

'Yes,' Aliah confirmed.

'Swear it on the goddess.'

'I swear on the goddess I will not use my weapons on any of your people, except in defence.'

That brought a smile. 'Fair enough.'

The bed was comfortable enough, and Megan left her a jug of water and a chamber pot. So Aliah had a reasonably comfortable night. Though try as she might, she could not rest once the sun shone through the small window above her. She took the last of Healer Goodwin's medicine, hoping it would relax her and let her fall back asleep. Today it seemed to have the opposite effect. Whether she liked it or not—and she did not—she was awake.

Rolling up her bed, she made a large cushion against the wall, then went through some stretching and sword exercises—the ones she could do in such a confined space. After a short time she was sweating and her body was tired. She took it as a good sign she wanted to exercise, but it was frustrating she was so weakened by her recent illness.

Then she had nothing to do but wait. For the first time in her life she wished she had a book handy. She wanted to read some more about Carsten and try and work out why it was suddenly so important for them to invade Aria. From her memory she knew they were not exactly a peaceful nation, but to try and invade a different continent seemed unusual to her. If only she had paid more attention to affairs of state when she had the opportunity.

Smiling wryly she thought, *I am learning a lot on this journey. For all that I used to argue with my father that I did not need a husband to rule for me, I find that I am really most unprepared to rule alone.* She frowned. *Or am I unprepared because I knew I was not likely to rule and so there was no point to all that knowledge?*

As she debated in her head, deciding no matter what, she was going to start behaving a bit more like she intended to rule Aria at some future point, the door opened and instead of Able, Megan entered. It was a welcome sight for Aliah as it meant she was earning Boss and his crew's trust.

'Come, be quick. We have breakfast for you in the side room.' Megan stepped aside to let her out.

Well, almost all of his crew. Abel was waiting for her

on the other side of the door, hand on sword, just daring her to run. Instead, she inclined her head and said good morning to him as she walked demurely to the room she had been in last night. Able and Megan both followed her in, and Able took his position by the door.

'Don't mind him.' Megan glanced towards the door as she sat down to eat with Aliah. 'He takes a long time to trust. Besides, he is there mostly for our security. Eat Your Highness,' she said as she tucked into her own meal.

'Your Highness.' Able snorted. 'We don't even know if she is a high anything yet.'

Aliah chose to ignore him and sat in the chair she had used the night before, sitting at right angles to Megan. 'Please, just call me Aliah.'

'Oh, but I couldn't.' Megan blushed.

'But you must,' Aliah insisted. 'For your sake as well as mine, no one can know who I am. Also, my friends call me Aliah in private, and I believe I have you to thank for your father giving me a hearing last night, rather than turning me over to the authorities, so I am sure we count as friends.'

There was a snort from behind again. This time Aliah turned around and raised at questioning brow at Able. 'Boss would never have given you over to that miserable excuse for a wizard. He is up to something, and Boss would not have let him have his worst enemy.'

'Oh.' Aliah was a bit deflated. 'I am sorry, I must have misread the situation. I thought Boss believed me and was merely waiting to confirm my story.'

'Able.' Megan's voice came as a warning. Able glowered back at her but said nothing.

BEGINNINGS

'What is going on?' she asked Megan.

Megan merely told her to eat her breakfast; things would be sorted later. Now the bread and cheese felt like sawdust in Aliah's mouth. She had thought she made friends last night, but now she was not so sure. Was she still in danger?

'How is your father going to prove my story? And what happens to me if he cannot?' Aliah asked Megan.

'Don't you be worrying about that. He has his ways.' Megan carried on eating as if there was nothing amiss.

Aliah took a sip of tea and looked around the room. Although it was morning the curtains were still drawn. She rose and went over to open them.

'Please, don't,' Megan said. 'If you want to look out, peak through the gap, but we don't want people looking in here.'

Suddenly Aliah did not want to see what was outside. Megan's tone of voice told her it was nothing good.

'Are they still looking for the boy?' Aliah asked as she paced round the room.

'They were out all last night,' Able said from the doorway. 'In the main town mostly. The wizard is sleeping in a room upstairs now. But the local soldiers and his hired help are doing a quick sweep outside the walls in the new town now.'

'Oh.' Aliah sat down again, her appetite mostly gone.

'He will be safe,' Megan assured her. 'He is with a friend of ours.'

There was a knock at the door and a young boy came in and whispered to Able. Able mumbled something in return, then said, 'You had best clear up in here then.'

The boy picked up a tray by the door and began clearing away the breakfast things, studiously not looking at Aliah. With the table cleared Able left the room and returned moments later with an extra chair, which he placed by the door. 'Looks like we are going to be here for some time,' Aliah said. 'Would it be possible for me to use the privy and wash up a little?'

'The privy is fine, but washing up will have to wait,' Megan told her. She led the way out of the room with Able following behind Aliah. Megan checked the courtyard behind the inn before letting Aliah out to the privy. Able stayed by the door and Megan walked out with her, advising her not to lock the door as she would hold it to from the outside. It seemed they did not trust her enough to even have privacy.

Aliah was readjusting her clothing when the door opened and Megan rushed in through a small gap. 'Sorry, stomach. May be some time,' she said through the gap as she firmly shut the door and locked it. She put her finger too her lips, warning Aliah not to speak, then made gagging sounds that would have made most children proud.

Megan continued her mock gagging for some time, pausing in between to whisper that one of the mercenaries had been heading towards the privy. Finally there was a knock on the door. Two quick knocks, a gap then two more. Megan poked her head out, grabbed Aliah by the arm, and hauled her back across the yard and into the corridor behind Able.

As the door closed, Able pushed the two of them into the storeroom Aliah had stayed the night in, pulling the door to but not closing it completely behind him. After a short time Aliah could just see a figure emerge through the gap.

BEGINNINGS

'Out of my way,' The man commanded, curling his lips at Able. Able moved to stand in front of the gap, blocking the man's view, and Aliah's as well. But she had seen enough.

'Have you changed your mind about telling me where the boy went? I will pay good gold for the information. Enough to set you and your wife up for life.'

Aliah could not be sure, but she thought Able shuddered as the wizard spoke to him.

'I was with your soldiers most of the night, as you well know. So how could I know where he has gone?'

'When I capture him, if I find out that you knew anything I will make what little life you have left very unpleasant,' the wizard spat at Able.

Megan squeezed Aliah's hand and it was then she realised Megan was the wife the wizard spoke of. Boss' crew were obviously his family and friends, so he had a lot to lose by keeping her hidden. Why would he risk so much? Aliah moved, intending to give herself up, not sure she could bear the responsibility of so many lives. But Megan pulled her back and shook her head, as if she had read her intentions.

Finally the wizard left, and Able spat on the floor after him as if clearing a bad taste from his mouth. He opened the door and the three of them continued back to the front room.

As Aliah entered her attention went immediately to the large pot of milky coffee on the table, a drink common to this area, and two men seated drinking. Boss was in the chair he had been in last night. The chair Megan had been sitting in was occupied by a bearded man who

Vivienne Lee Fraser

looked to be about sixty, except for his blue eyes, which seemed to look right through her. He seemed familiar, but she could not immediately place him.

'Come in. Sit down.' Boss indicated the chair in front of the window. 'Megan, you can go now.'

'I don't think so,' she said as she sat down in the chair Aliah had vacated. Able sat in the seat he had placed by the door, and Aliah had no choice but to stand, or sit in the remaining chair. She chose to sit.

'Megan,' Boss rumbled at his daughter, clearly displeased.

'I noticed her in the wagon. I covered for her when others noticed something amiss. I have aided you in keeping her a secret. I will not desert her to you now.' She folded her arms in front of her chest and stared her father down.

Boss chuckled and caught the other man's eye. 'You should be pleased you have never had children. I have a son who just wants to stay home with his mother and run the farm, and a daughter who would take on any man.'

'You have been truly blessed by the goddess.' The man smiled at Boss, seeing through his bluster at the pride he had in his children.

'And before you ask, she is probably who she says she is. I have one last test though.' His attention moved to Aliah. 'The royal family have a secret code they use to senior advisors and officers when they are in trouble but cannot say so openly. What is that code?'

Aliah looked around the room at the people she barely knew. From childhood it had been drilled into her that she should only use this code in extreme situations, and only with people in the king's employ who she could trust. Her first reaction was to say nothing, as she could compromise the whole royal family if this information fell into the wrong hands. Yet her natural instincts had not been so good lately. She needed help, and she needed to trust someone. Also the way the man asked the question it was as though he knew the answer already. She stared at him, trying to place his face, but could not. He merely raised an eyebrow back at her. She took a breath, tucked a stray strand of hair behind her ear, decision made.

'Black Swan,' Aliah said.

The man's face showed nothing, he merely nodded at Boss Allum. Boss focused his gaze on Aliah, 'So, Your Highness, we know what you have told us is the truth as you believe it to be. We also know from talk in the tavern last night that an invasion fleet is preparing to sail from Carsten. This reinforces your story. There is a missing piece of the puzzle that perhaps you do not know, and Walter here can provide that.' Boss indicated the other man.

Aliah also turned to him, and stopped. A moment ago she would have sworn the man in front of her was sixty—maybe even older. Now he looked somewhere in his forties. Something was tickling in the back of her brain now. She knew him, she had seen him round the castle. He had been clean-shaven. He had been in wizard robes. But he was not Walter. He was … he was … 'Walton,' she blurted out. 'You are Walton, the wizard who went a bit crazy and had to give up running the wizard school and was sent out to work in the towns and villages.'

The man in front of her shook his head. 'Crazy? That is a bit much.' He shrugged his shoulders. 'I am now

Walter. I will never use that other name again and I would appreciate it if you do not, Highness. I changed my name when I left the wizard order. I am now an outcast, some would even believe a traitor. There is sure to be a price on my head. So if you would not mind, keep that name to yourself.'

Aliah was shocked. No wizard was allowed to leave the order and keep their magic. Especially if they were as gifted as Walton was. The wizard order regulated the use of magic, and made sure it was only used for the good of the people. Unregulated magic was an abomination. 'I am sorry.' Aliah rose. 'But I cannot work with a rogue wizard. I thank you for your help. But I must find my own way home now.'

'Reacting rather than thinking again.' Boss looked keenly at her. 'That is no way to make important decisions.'

Aliah stopped, then sat back down. Boss had a very annoying habit of speaking to her conscience. 'I am not sure what you can say that will change my mind. But I will hear you out.' She folded her hands on the table and stared at Walton ... Walter.

'I am not going to justify my actions to you. I had good reasons for what I did. What I will do is ask you to think on something, and this was something I did not think about myself until recently, so take your time. Magic is not limited to men only, yet there are no women attending school on the Wizard Isle, and there are no women on the wizard council. Recently the council started turning away all but wealthy students. There have always been mages outside the control of the Council of Wizards. Although it is said to be illegal, unless they use their gift to harm others, magic users are left alone. So you could say the regulation of magic, and the wizard council itself, are political constructs and have very little to do with the safety of the realm and managing all users of magic.'

Aliah looked at him, mouth open. Then shut her mouth because she was sure she looked like a half-wit. Why hadn't she thought about that before? Women were born with magic. What happened to them? Women like Amelia. And they were turning away boys from the wizard school?

'Is that why you left, because you thought all boys should be trained?' she asked him.

'No.' He shook his head. 'That happened after I left. But I was not surprised. I left because I realised that the wizard council in the hands of the wrong people was not merely a political construct but a tool that could be used to destabilise the country. At the moment it is in the hands of people who do not have Aria's best interests at heart and who are working for their own gain. They are involving themselves in things they should not. When I spoke out about this I was denounced and everyone was told I had a breakdown. I was forced to resign my post and take a position in the community. While I worked, I witnessed the impact the new council was having on people, and I could no longer be a part of it.'

Thoughts raced through Aliah's head and she closed her eyes, trying to put them in order. The Head of the Council had died, and a new head had been elected. Not long after, her father's chief advisor, a wizard, had a heart attack. The council had appointed a new advisor, Wizard Millard, and it had been he who had spoken most strongly in favour of Aliah being married to the

King of Carsten. It was he who she most wished to avoid before seeing her father.

She opened her eyes and looked at Walter. 'I can see this from your point of view. I also have some concerns about the current wizard's council. I am happy to work with you if you are willing to help me. But what I do not understand is why you are all willing to risk so much to help me.'

Boss and Walter looked at each other. Boss broke away first.

'My reasoning is simple. Evil happens when good people stand by and do nothing. There is something evil going on in Aria. I cannot place my finger on it, but I know it is there. Me and mine will fight evil where we find it. And we fight along side others spread through Aria.' He sat back in his chair indicating he was finished.

'Thank you for your honesty.' Aliah now waited for Walter to answer.

'I have very specific reasons. I want to see the wizard council restored to what it was, and I believe what is happening to you may be part of the corruption that runs through it.'

'Is that it? Or are you going to tell me how you think this is all linked?' Aliah looked Walter in the eye.

'Will knowing help you?' he asked in return.

Aliah shrugged. 'Maybe not. But I like to know who my enemies are. And maybe it is something I can bring to the attention of my father when I get to see him.'

'Your father has already been told. He chose to believe the official version of the truth.'

Gritting her teeth in frustration, Aliah tried to keep

her voice calm. 'Combined with what I have to tell him, he may change his mind. Even if he does not, maybe I will be able to do something about it when I am queen.'

'If you ever make it to be queen,' Walter retorted.

'If that is in question then I definitely need to know,' Aliah threw back.

'Just tell her already,' Boss interrupted. 'We do not have time for this arguing.'

Walter shrugged his shoulders and sat back in his chair. 'I went to the Wizard Isles when I was about ten, and spent many years there. For the most part I was happy to live there and serve my king and country. But a little over five years ago, my mentor, the Grand Wizard, died unexpectedly. It was said to be from a brain disorder, but I knew it could not be true as he had always been sound of health. So I did some digging. From the evidence I gathered I suspected he had been poisoned. I confirmed this when I over-heard two other council members planning what would happen next now they had rid themselves of their opposition.'

'It was an enlightening conversation, one that resulted in me learning there was a faction within the wizard's congress who had planned a different type of government for Aria. One where wizards took their rightful place as leaders of the people.'

'Their plan was simple but devious. They were to place a puppet as Grand Wizard, then begin moving the kingdom towards a war they could not win. When the royal family was removed and it looked like all was lost, the Council of Wizards would reluctantly overcome their restrictions on using battle magic and save the day, thus earning the support of the people to continue keeping them safe and ruling as wizards rightfully should.'

Aliah looked as though she was going to interrupt, but Walter held up his hand, 'Just a minute more, then you can ask questions. So, the new Grand Wizard was elected. Gregory is a noble man with more of an interest in magical research than the politics required to govern a diverse group of men. But he has a good heart and always puts the interests of the kingdom first, so he was confirmed in his position by the king.'

'When I took my fears about my mentor's death to Gregory, he listened to his advisors rather than me. I was quickly sidelined and told I was being foolish. That was the truth. I was foolish. I moved before I had concrete proof against those who plotted against the crown. My position became compromised. Against all advice I would not stop my investigations. Finally I was removed from my position as head teacher of the initiates least I subvert new wizard trainees, and I was exiled to work as a healer in a remote village.'

'I carried out my work diligently for a few months. Then I found out one of the men who was plotting the downfall of the king had been appointed as his chief advisor after the current advisor had had a heart attack. I realised I could no longer serve in an organisation that was so corrupt.'

Aliah was sitting there with her mouth open in disbelief. She quickly closed it. She went to say something to refute these preposterous claims, but held her tongue while her thoughts settled. She knew this timeline to be correct. She herself did not trust Millard. It was his lackey, Gaius,

BEGINNINGS

she had seen in the hallway before, and she knew no good reason to trust him as he had made his contempt of her obvious on numerous occasions.

'So ... I was to be sent away, my family was to be killed, and all so the wizards could run Aria?' Aliah asked, trying hard to keep the skepticism from her voice.

Walter seemed unconcerned with Aliah's lack of trust. 'It is the truth, but I did not expect you to believe me.'

'I don't disbelieve you,' Aliah said, thoughtfully. 'It is just a lot to take in.'

'If I may,' Boss interrupted. 'We have confirmed much of Walter's story through other sources. In fact, we believe the king's advisor, Millard, might actually be working with Carsten to set this war up. We are not sure of the exact details. But we are concerned.'

Aliah frowned. 'You know a lot for a farmer who dabbles in transporting goods.'

'Not all people are what they seem.' Boss smiled as if he had a secret to tell. 'I was a captain in the guard until I brought a farm and settled with my Ann. We had a family and I started running caravans on the side to make a bit of extra money. I began to pick up information as I travelled, and some of it was very worrying. Along with some like minded people, I helped form a bit of a network to share what we knew, and now we have a group of people ready to act in the defence of our country.'

It was Aliah's turn to smile. 'It seems like I was very lucky to pick your wagon to stow away on. What do we do now? I need to get to my father.'

'Leave it with us,' Boss said. 'There are further searches today for both you and the boy travelling with us. Guess you don't know any reason why they would want to find him?'

Aliah shook her head, Seamus was better off left out of all this.

Boss raised his eyebrows, but did not voice what was on his mind. 'We have had the storeroom cleared and when it is safe you will be taken up to Megan and Abel's room. You can tidy yourself up and change into some local clothes. We have some planning to do, but we have a way to smuggle you out of Duncameron, hopefully tomorrow evening. We need to get to work though and start shifting our goods before someone asks what we have been doing with our day. Tonight we will finalise our plans.'

Conversation time was clearly over. Megan and Able bundled Aliah out of the room and up the stairs. Safe in a large, simple room Aliah was able to bathe and change into local clothing. Checking her pack and sword were safely stowed, she had nothing else to do. The boy brought a midday meal up, and he had thoughtfully included a book. Unfortunately it was a book of hero's tales and bedtime stories. Not really to Aliah's taste. She had grown out of childish tales like *The Wizard and Warrior* years ago. Based on a prophecy, she used to enjoy reading how the two young men saved the world from disaster after disaster using a mixture of magic and muscle. Still, she had nothing better to do, so she skimmed through some of the stories, only to be woken by the boy bringing her some supper and telling her to be ready to leave in about a candle-mark.

Walter came for her not long after. He led her through the back door of the inn to the town gates, then through the winding back streets of town to the industrial district. The streets were in utter darkness and there was no one about. Walter explained this was because the soldiers had imposed a curfew until she and the boy were found.

Quietly he led her through the door of a warehouse that was stuffed full with shanks of wool hanging from racks. Aliah smiled to herself, remembering how she had escaped ship into a warehouse full of bales of wool. Wool seemed to be a theme for her. Brushing through aisle after aisle of wool they came to a staircase and Walter led her upwards. There were two doors off the landing. He opened the one on the left, which was clearly used as a small office. The windows had been shuttered and a bed had been set up on the floor.

'There is food and water on the table, and I have left you some candles and books. There is to be a house-to-house search tomorrow. It is unlikely they will come around here, but it will be best to keep quiet during the day so no one suspects this room is in use. The manager who uses the office next door of course knows you are here, and should anything happen you are to look to him for help. He has not had an assistant for a while and no one will think it strange this door is locked.'

'I am to stay here tonight?' Aliah asked, looking around.

'Yes.' Walter confirmed. 'And all of tomorrow. After the search is over and the factory has closed for the day, someone will come and get you.' He busied himself lighting a candle for her so she would not have to spend the night in the dark.

The last thing Aliah wanted was to spend all that time alone, but she had little choice if she wanted help to escape Duncameron and get home to Bannock.

'Are you fine for me to lock you in?' Walter seemed a little concerned.

Aliah shrugged. 'I guess so.'

'Right. See you tomorrow evening then.'

The door shut behind him with the snick of the lock being activated. She was alone once again. She had never spent so much time by herself as she had since leaving the confines of Bannock Castle. It was something she was getting used to but she did miss Seamus' company.

Aliah was already up and doing some limbering exercises when she heard the first workers arrive the next day. She had packed her gear away and laid out her food earlier. When she heard noises downstairs all she had to do was retire to her bed and spend the rest of the day eating and reading. Not long after she heard the workers stop for the midday meal, she started to doze, but was woken by the noise of someone pulling at the door handle as if they were trying different keys in the lock. The sound was followed by voices.

Quietly, she pulled her bed and everything on it between the window and desk, out of view from the door. She crouched down and hoped everything was hidden from sight, then she spied her pack and sword behind the door where Walter had left them the night before.

But it was too late, the key was turning in the lock and the door was opening.

'As you can see, this room has not been in use for

BEGINNINGS

some time.' The door partway opened and someone entered the room.

'Fine,' a second voice said. 'No, wait, is that a story book on the desk? An odd thing to have in an office.'

'It is indeed a story book,' the first voice said. 'It belongs to my old assistant. He left it behind and he did not leave a forwarding address for me to send it to. I have not had the heart to be rid of it as it seemed to be special to him. Really, it was strange that he left it behind.'

'Mmm. Any more rooms up here?'

'Yes, on the next level up. This way.' The door closed and the lock clicked and there was a rattle as the key was removed.

Aliah let out her breath. No longer sleepy, she sat leaning against the window, willing the time to pass more quickly and marvelling at how much of her time on this adventure had been spent waiting around for something to happen. Boredom soon got the better of her and she eventually fell asleep.

12
ESCAPE BELOW

Walter led Seamus out of the house and into the shadows of the darkened street. He stopped, muttered a few words in front of his door, then led him on through windy streets into what appeared to be the poorer section of town. Seamus followed silently, keeping to the shadows, until Walter signalled for him to stop. He waited while Walter crossed the street and disappeared into the courtyard behind a building. Hand on one of his knives, Seamus looked around for any movement that indicated they had been followed.

A few minutes later Walter signalled for him to cross the street. He did so as quickly as possible, nearly jumping out of his skin when a dog barked in a nearby building. Waiting, a few moments later the dog's owner yelled for it to stop jumping at shadows. Seamus carried on and Walter led him to the yard at the back of what looked to be a dye works. When they were inside he shut the gate and walked over to a large metal grate.

Walter motioned for Seamus to help him open it up, and as he did the stench released made him gag. Two figures emerged from the shadows and Seamus instinctively got ready to fight. Walter shook his head and motioned the figures over. It was the young boy who had been helping him over the last few days. He had a cloth wrapped around his mouth and nose. His companion was also similarly covered, but Seamus would know her anywhere. Aliah. He looked at Walter, who was clearly watching him to see what his reaction would be, so he feigned nonchalance.

The two figures approached and the boy offered Seamus and Walter coverings for their faces. As Seamus tied his he realised there was camphor and something else on the material to help deal with the smells of the sewer.

'Keep this tight,' Walter whispered. 'It not only helps with the smell but will help filter some of the sewer gases, which can be deadly if too much is inhaled.'

Aliah had kept her attention on the hole in the ground as she approached, and had not yet noticed Seamus. It gave him time to sort through his conflicting feelings over seeing Aliah again. Relieved that she was all right. But his overwhelming feeling was one of anger. He was angry at how she had treated him, and angry that she was again to be his travelling companion.

He tied on his mask and decided he would just ignore her.

Aliah had been surprised when the boy from the inn arrived at her door, but glad it was finally time to go. She could not believe such a young child was to get her out of Duncameron.When he said they would be meeting up with Walter she realised he was just a messenger and was happy to leave with him. They left the warehouse and went through a gate to the courtyard next door, which seemed to belong to some sort of dye works.

From the shadow of the buildings she could see two figures were already there, but her attention was focused on the drain they were to go through into the sewers. As they approached she could smell the odours waft up from below.

I cannot go down there. If the rats don't kill me the smell will. She kept her thoughts to herself though, merely wrinkling her nose under the cover of the wrapping round her face and looked up to greet Walter. Instead, she came face to face with Seamus.

She was so shocked she took a step back and nearly fell into the sewer. It looked like Walter was smiling knowingly under his mask as he watched her right herself. Seamus looked away, not even acknowledging her presence. It hurt, but what else could she expect after the way she had behaved? Once out of Duncameron, they could take their separate paths, and that would be that. Still, that loss of comradeship saddened her.

The boy nipped away and returned with four unlit torches. He handed one to each of them, and began the descent through the mouth of the grate into the sewer. Walter motioned for Seamus to follow, then Aliah, then he bought up the rear, pulling the metal grate over behind them as he climbed down. When they were all in the tunnel Walter spoke a word and his torch took light, another word and the one in the boy's hand was also giving off a smoky light.

'Right, we don't have much time, so I will keep it brief. Young Pauley here will lead; he knows these tunnels like the back of his hand. I will be rear guard. The flames will light our way but also, hopefully, keep the worst of the rats at bay.'

Aliah shuddered, she could already hear them scrabbling around and the thought of them anywhere near her made her want to scream in panic. But she kept her mouth firmly closed, muttering over and over to herself, 'I will get through this, it is only a short time.'

'You two, keep your torches dry as we might need them later. Right! Off we go.'

'Wait!' Seamus stopped them, 'Firstly, is it safe for me to be walking around, you know, broadcasting my magic?'

Walter chuckled. 'Your broadcast is now a mere trickle, and it is easy for me to deflect prying eyes from noticing it. Someone would have to be scrying specifically for magic users to notice us. And if they were doing that, we would be in trouble most definitely. And at the moment I can detect no such activity. So can we go now?'

BEGINNINGS

'And what if we get split up?' Seamus asked.

'I would strongly recommend against that,' Walter answered. 'Pauley is the only one of us who knows these tunnels and if we lose him we could be lost down here for days.'

'Oh,' was all Seamus said in response, but Aliah noticed a frown crease his brow.

'Any more questions?' Walter looked at them. 'Right, no? Well let us be going. The sooner we are out of the city the safer we will be.'

Aliah's heart lurched but she forced herself to put one foot in front of the other, keeping her eyes on Seamus' back directly in front of her, trying not to think about the smell or the creatures she could feel running over her feet. They followed Pauley through the tunnels for what seemed like a number of candle-marks. Aliah keeping her growing sense of panic from breaking out by chanting her mantra and ignoring the scratching and scrabbling. No one spoke until Walter quietly asked from the back, 'How much longer Pauley?'

'About half a candle-mark,' the young boy answered.

'We don't have that much time,' Walter said. 'We have a scryer working. They will find us within a few heartbeats if we keep this pace. We need to run.'

With that warning Pauley picked up the pace to a jog, and they all followed his lead. At the sound of voices ahead Walter dimmed the torches until they were just a small glow.

In the near darkness the slimy water splashed up Aliah's clothing. A rat squeaked as her foot landed on its body. She slipped and had to grasp Seamus to stop herself from falling into the sludge. The thought of joining the rat in the sewer water made her want to throw up. As she regained her footing and Seamus readied himself to lead them on, she realised they could no longer see the dim glow of Pauley's torch. Aliah moved to continue, but Seamus held her back.

'Just wait. Pauley will realise we are not with him and come back to find us.' It was the first time he had spoken to her since they entered the tunnels.

'But we are being followed, we need to keep moving.' She tugged at the arm that restrained her.

'Can you, just for once, take someone else's advice?' Seamus snapped back.

'He is right.' Aliah had forgotten Walter was still with them. 'Without Pauley we could be lost in the sewers for days.'

They waited for some time. They could hear footsteps echo in the sewers. Walter doused his light, then made a small mage flame so Pauley would know where they were. As footsteps came nearer, Walter doused the flame and Aliah's anxiety levels rose. She moved as if to start running. Seamus grabbed her arm and pulled her back.

'You will get us all caught,' he said through gritted teeth.

'I have shielded us while we are stationary,' Walter whispered. 'We should be all right unless someone walks right into us.'

As if his words had willed it a dark figured turned down the tunnel in front and headed straight towards them. Aliah held her breath and tried not to make a sound. The figure was getting closer. A body length away. Half a body length. If he reached out his hand he could touch Seamus. Then he stopped. Another figure appeared in front of them at the tunnel mouth.

'We heard something down this way. Come on.'

'I am sure there is something down here,' the man in front of them responded.

'It's nothing. *Come on.*'

The figure hesitated, then decided it was best to follow his mate. Aliah waited until they were out of sight before letting out her breath. It seemed like only a moment later there were more footsteps coming closer. This time from behind them. Aliah held still, but this time the feel of something scuttling over her foot broke her concentration. She bit back a scream, but a moan still escaped her mouth. She froze, mortified that she had given away their position. She got ready to run.

'I have sent them through a maze of tunnels. Should be a while 'til they are back this way.'

Aliah let out a breath she had not even known she was holding. It was Pauley.

'Come on, this way.'

Walter sent a mage light after Pauley so they could follow him. They all ran as fast as they could for the next half a candle-mark. With her lungs burning they finally made it out the sewer entrance into a bubbling stream. Pauley led them up-steam back towards the city. He paused. 'You can wash off and change here. Just over there is the rendezvous.' He pointed to a group of trees. He went to turn back, but Walter grabbed his arm.

'I am sorry lad, but it is not safe in the sewers and the gates are long closed, even for those who know how to pay their way. It is not safe for you to go back home now. You will have to come with us.'

'But, Walter, my family will be worried. And I have to be at work in the morning.' Pauley looked distressed.

'I am sorry, son. Your family knew it was a possibility you would have to leave with us. We will get word back to them that you are all right as soon as we can. But for now, you need to clean your clothes, and hopefully they will dry by morning. I have a cape you can wrap yourself in until then.'

'I have a spare trousers and shirt for him, no sense in risking disease with keeping any of these,' Seamus interrupted. 'They are not local clothing, but should anyone ask, we can say we found him wandering dressed in strange clothes.'

'Most helpful, young man. And as we are unlikely to see anybody the way we are going, it will not matter too much that they are not local.'

Seamus paused to find the trousers, then returned to changing into his clean clothes and boots. When he had finished he grabbed his and Aliah's clothes and began digging a hole to bury them in.

Pauley look mutinous as he hitched up Seamus' too big trousers and put on the shirt he was passed. Still, he scrubbed his boots until there was no trace of the sewer mud on them and Seamus tied them onto his pack to dry. Walter found some cloth to bind his feet in to see them through to the meeting place. Seamus buried the last of their clothing and covered the hole he had dug. When they were ready to travel Walter hurried them to their rendezvous through the trees nearby.

'They are still in the sewers looking for us. I have

placed a blocking spell at the exit we came through that will take a strong wizard to detect, so we have some time before they start looking outside the town. But we do need to be away as soon as possible.'

In the copse Walter led them to, there were four horses and a rather sun-dried looking man of an indeterminate age. He wore the leather clothing of the mountain people, with a broad hat that covered most of his face.

'You are late, and one too many,' he said, abruptly, to Walter.

'Slight change of plan with him,' Walter answered. 'Those who pursue us are already in the sewers. He has to come. This possibility was foreseen and accounted for.'

'He can ride with the girl.' The man pulled himself into his saddle and waited for the others to mount. All but Pauley had ridden before and there was a look of terror on his face as Walter lifted him up behind Aliah.

'Just hold on to me and we will be fine,' Aliah encouraged him, and immediately there was a vice-like grip around her waist. 'I need to breathe though,' she chided him and his grip loosened ever so slightly.

'We have one, maybe two candle-marks until it is too light to travel,' their guide told them as he looked at Walter. 'You know what to do?'

Walter nodded as their guide set off at a fast pace, Aliah following, with Seamus behind her, and Walter at the rear. They headed back towards the city to the base of the Highland Mountains and it was not long before they started their ascent. Aliah looked back to see Walter a little behind them, muttering and sweeping his arm. It took a minute, then she laughed to herself. 'Just removing the tracks.' She relaxed a little. One less way for their enemies to find them.

Tired and sore, they finally dismounted just as the sun was coming up. They took care of the horses first, removing their saddles, rubbing them down, then feeding them. Their guide said to let them wander, they did not like being tied up. As hill ponies they would not move too far from the stream running through their campsite. They set up their camp in the lee of a rock face, and their guide built a fire and started cooking porridge with dried fruit and nuts for their breakfast. Aliah went to fill a kettle with water for some tea, she was grateful she still had some of Amelia's leaves in her pack.

When their meal was ready they all sat down to eat, and Aliah expected introductions. When none were made she pointedly looked at their guide and said, 'We have not been introduced?' Before she could go any further their guide held up his hand.

'We do not do it that way.' He looked at Walter, expecting him to explain.

'We have contracted our friend to take us safely through the mountains. He is a member of a very old brotherhood who live as hermits in the remote mountain valleys. They take on special contracts from time to time to supplement their income in times of hardship. They know only the people who arrange their contracts and make payments. Our guide is honour bound to fulfil his contract and only that. We do not need to know him and he does not need or want to know us, or what we are doing. If you need to speak to him he goes by the name of Namate, which means guide in his language.'

BEGINNINGS

Aliah knew her surprise must have been written on her face, as Walter spoke again. 'Not all who work with us are dedicated to our cause, but be aware we carefully consider any alliances we make. The Namate are an honourable group, and their agent has made sure we are not doing anything that would affect the karma of this Namate while he carries out his duties. This is a contract that benefits both groups and hurts neither.'

How strange the world outside the palace is, Aliah thought to herself. Although she was no stranger to political alliances they did not seem as odd as this agreement was to her.

'We must sleep now,' Namate explained. 'We move as soon as the sun goes down.' And with that, he took the blanket from his horse and went over to sleep by the stream, close to his horses.

Walter set up another horse blanket and made a bed by the fire for Pauley, who was just about dead on his feet. He, Aliah, and Seamus crawled into their swags. Aliah had to admit she was almost as tired as Pauley looked. Although she was now well over her illness she was by no means back to full strength. Still, as it appeared Seamus was to be travelling with them for a little while she knew she had something to do before she allowed herself to rest. Her stomach clenched as she sat up and leaned over to shake Seamus.

'What.'

'Seamus ...' she paused, unsure what to say next.

'Yes?' He still had not rolled over to look at her.

What could she say to make up for running out on him without a word, and leaving him to sort things with

Healer Goodwin? No mere words could make that better.

'I am sorry. I acted on impulse without thinking about how it would affect you or others. I will try my best not to let it happen again.'

Seamus still did not move.

Aliah sighed. It was all that she could do. It was up to Seamus now. With a heavy heart, she laid back down in her sleeping bag and tried to sleep.

'It seems as if the fates keep throwing us together,' he said without rolling over. 'But we are travelling companions only now. I am not sure I can trust you more than that.'

'Fair enough.' What else could she say? It was up to her to make amends with actions. But she felt even more lonely knowing she had lost his friendship.

The smell of meat cooking over a newly built fire awoke Aliah. Namate was cooking some kind of animal for the evening meal, so Aliah got up to see what she could do to help. She stowed her swag and went to the stream to freshen up and get water for everyone.

When she returned, Seamus was performing some sort of sword practice without a sword. She watched him for a while, finally plucking up the courage to go over and see whether travelling companions talked to each other.

'Do you want to borrow my sword to practice with?' she asked him.

'Not sword practice,' he said without breaking his stride.

She watched him some more. 'It amazes me how you can be so good on your feet, but the minute you put a

BEGINNINGS

sword in your hand it all goes wrong,' Aliah mused out loud. Seamus started to smile then stopped himself.

Aliah watched some more. It dawned on her what he was actually doing. He was using the formwork of sword practice for some sort of unarmed attack and defence. She continued to watch him and when he moved to defence she got up and faced him, starting with the attack forms to match what he was doing. Seamus faltered for a moment when she joined him, but continued a moment later.

'No, if you do that move like this it works better.'

Aliah followed him, then they repeated the moves with his change. It did indeed work much better. They switched, and with some more adjustments by Seamus, Aliah was able to pick up the defensive role. By the time they finished, Aliah was out of breath and ready for dinner. They had not spoken, but Aliah hoped the ice between them had melted a little.

They ate quickly and while Aliah and Pauley helped break camp, Walter spent some time with Seamus explaining to him some magic training he wanted him to do while they were riding. After his lesson, Seamus buried their rubbish and they were ready to leave. As they were riding away, Walter spoke some words and waved his arm around the area all trace of their having been at the campsite was removed.

For two nights they rode through the mountain trails. Seamus barely spoke to Aliah, but was happy to practice the unarmed combat he had developed with her when he was not having magic lessons with Walter. With no one following them, their journey became monotonous, so much so that Pauley fell asleep against her back for most of the night. They did not talk much as Walter seemed reluctant to discuss anything in front of Namate. As they rode closer to Castle Bannock Aliah's stomach begin to tighten. She knew she had to talk to her father, but she was unsure of what sort of reception she would get. Would he be angry with her, or would he be pleased she was safe? Would he believe her when she told him what had been happening?

When she left the Castle her father had been proud of her for taking on responsibilities for the kingdom. He would not know her escorts had become her captors, although he would have been concerned about her companions being asked to leave the ship. Would he be angry at her for disobeying him and placing the future of the kingdom at risk? And that was even if she could get in to see him. Walter said he had a way, but could he get passed the legion of advisors who surrounded her father whose express role was to keep others out. As princess, she could always get some time with her father, but she would not be able to play that role until after she had actually seen him. Having no one to discuss her fears with meant they began to take on mammoth proportions in her head.

Halfway through the fourth night Namate stopped them at a fork in the path. 'That way is your way.' He pointed to the fork on his right. 'This way is mine. When you get outside Bannock let the horses go. They will find their way back. My part of the arrangement is met, your part will be met when the horses return to our home.'

'I agree your part of our contract is concluded,' Walter said formally, and with that their guide nudged his horse

BEGINNINGS

and headed off.

'How odd,' Aliah murmured.

'It is their way,' Walter said. 'For them, this is solely a contract. They want no thanks and no part of our lives. They have no care but for their own community. Come, we need to get to the foot of the mountains before daybreak if our plan is to work.'

13
BANNOCK

The four weary travellers steered their horses down the path their guide had set them on. There was no more talking than there had been the previous nights as they were all so tired from the constant travel and having to sleep through the day. A little before sunrise, they reached the bottom of the mountain range. Aliah startled when Walter led them to two wagons and some goats being minded by an elderly man and woman who, from their dress, were farmers on their way to market.

Vivienne Lee Fraser

'Hello.' Walter greeted them cheerfully.

'Come, we don't have much time before sun-up.' The other man was a little brisk in his manner. His careworn face seemed tense, and his eyes darted around as if worried someone might come upon them.

'We have ridden long friend, do we not have time to break our fast?' Walter asked.

'Mona has hotcakes with honey for you and fresh milk. You can eat as we travel. But we need to be back on that road by sun-up to avoid suspicion and arrive at the gates at our normal time. Also, I will feel better when we are travelling in the safety of market goers. There have been a large number of wizards on the road this last six-day and I would not like to think what they would do should they find us here. It would be a little hard to explain.'

Walter sighed. 'All right. Seamus and Aliah feed and water the horses, then set them free. Pauley, come here, we have clothes for you to change into. You two can get changed into yours when you are done with the horses.'

They each went to their tasks, but Aliah had to say she was distracted by the smell of hotcakes. Mona quickly helped her change into a plain skirt and shirt similar to her own behind one of the wagons. When she emerged, she noticed Seamus wearing clothes similar to the man who had greeted them. Walter and Pauley too had been transformed into farm workers. She would hardly have recognised them and she knew them all. The large brimmed sunhats could be mostly responsible for that. Her sword and Seamus' knives were stowed beneath some turnips, and then the farmer climbed up on the seat of his cart. They were ready to go.

BEGINNINGS

'I am Farmer Nobb and this is my wife, Mona. I will drive one wagon and Walter will drive the other.' Aliah wondered whether this man knew who Walter really was, or had he been kept in the dark about his real identity? Surely he would not order him about that way if he knew Walter was a powerful wizard.

'I come to the markets here once a week, and today is my day. Normally I have farm workers ride with me, but today I have my brother and his children helping me as a treat for his eldest children. We are Uncle and Aunt to you. Try not to speak and try to look as though you are amazed by your first trip to Castle Bannock.'

'That won't be hard.' Pauley laughed. 'It is.' Aliah smiled, Pauley's good mood was infectious.

'When we get through the city gates you must continue with me to market and help set up. Not to do so will be noticed. Then you will be free to wander. I will tell you when. It is then that you will meet your contact to get you into the castle.'

'This is your plan to get us in to Bannock? You expect us to just walk in?' Seamus looked shocked.

'There are no secret entrances to the city boy. You go in through the gates or not at all,' Farmer Nobb said disdainfully. 'You can try getting in without our help, safer for us all round, but being in plain sight and with someone the guard knows is your best bet.'

Walter merely shrugged his shoulders. 'The choice is yours Seamus. You can come with us and help us get into the castle, or you can go on alone. Though you need to make your mind up quickly. We need to be on the move.'

So Seamus had been aiming to help them get into Bannock Castle. She hoped he was still prepared to, even knowing she was there.

Trying not to let it show how much it mattered to her that Seamus came with them, she walked over to the farmer's wife. 'I guess Pauley and I are helping with the goats?' She smiled at Mona, who smiled in return and gave each of them a wooden switch and showed them how to move the goats.

Seamus stood there gnawing on his lip, watching Aliah learn how to herd goats. The princess doing a goatherd's work. It made him smile a little.

He had to say Aliah seemed prepared to do whatever it took to get back to see her father, and he had been rather surprised to find her following someone else's plan to the letter these last few days. After her apology, he was no longer angry with her, but he was still wary of trusting her too much.

When he had first seen her, he realised what the package was Walter needed to get into the castle. At first he had decided he would leave them at Bannock. He no longer had an urge to help Aliah. If only it were that easy for him. His desire to be rid of Aliah warred with his conscience which said he should be doing everything he could to help his people in the upcoming war.

Then Aliah had apologised. It did not change everything, but he knew what it took her to admit she was wrong. He also respected the fact she had not pushed him to accept her apology, but had instead worked with him as a travelling companion and showed that she was now listening to others.

'What am I to do?' Seamus asked himself, grumpily.

'Why, you can lead my ox.' Farmer Nobb laughed. 'He likes to wander a bit and does a little better with someone walking beside him.'

Unaware he had spoken out loud, Seamus had to laugh at the farmer's answer. Of course he was to lead an ox into Bannock. It was all so utterly ridiculous he could not stop himself from laughing. That did not mean he was committing to help Aliah get into the Castle though. He was still definitely undecided on that.

Mona handed out hotcakes and flasks of cool milk for the travellers to eat and drink as they walked. Aliah could see Seamus' ox ate most of his share of hotcakes when the boy was not looking. It did nothing to improve Seamus' mood as they joined other farmers heading towards Bannock. He still mumbled to himself and frowned under his hat.

As they walked towards Castle Bannock they each took a turn riding in the back of a wagon catching up on the sleep they had lost riding through the night. Just as the sun came up, the castle came into view, magnificent sitting atop its rock, and a lump caught in Aliah's throat as she got her first view of home.

Farmer Nobb called for all hands on deck as the town walls and castle loomed closer. The oxen became jittery, and the goats seem intent on losing themselves in the crowds heading for market. Aliah caught Seamus' eye. 'Does this seem familiar?' she asked as they joined the queue of farmers attending the day's market. Seamus beamed a genuine smile for the first time that day as he remembered the first time they met. After that, his mood seemed to lighten. The queue was relatively short when they joined it, and it was not long before it was their turn to have their wagon's searched by the guard.

'Good day for it, Farmer Nobb,' the guard said as he took the entrance fee to the city and noted it down in a ledger.

'It's always a good day to make a sale,' the farmer responded as he made his mark.

'Not bringing any of your regulars today?'

'They have the day at home working the fields. I brought my brother and his family to help, and to let his young ones see the town.'

'Hope they enjoy the sights. Bannock is always fun the first time, and today's market seems especially busy.' The soldier waved them through.

On the other side of the gate the farmer led them through the main road towards the large market square. 'That was too easy,' Seamus murmured to Aliah.

'Just hiding in plain sight,' she whispered back. But a glimpse of black wizard robes and a familiar face made her stop, heart in throat. Gaius was in the town.

'What?' Seamus asked her. She did not want to answer, they had been getting on so well this last candle-mark; actually talking. But she had promised herself she would deal with him honestly and so she would.

'There was a wizard in Duncameron. I remember him

from my father's court. He was a nasty boy and he has grown into an even nastier man. I just saw him walk down that street. I am sure he is looking for me.'

'For us,' Seamus said. 'If he is who I think he is, then he was also looking for me. He made my stomach curdle. He was spreading some tale about us being the wizard and warrior from some old prophecy to scare people from helping or approaching us.'

Aliah went to laugh, but the serious look on Seamus' face stopped her. 'Some people actually believed it. Ask Pauley?'

'Come on, you two, we cannot stand about here gawping.' Walter moved them along. More quietly he said, 'I saw him too. In all this bustle he will be unlikely to find us. But we need to be wary.'

The main square was busy with farmers and merchants setting up for the twice-weekly markets. Tents were everywhere and people were hurrying to get set up before customers arrived. The market manager waved them over towards the fresh produce area and, as they walked past, he took a special interest in Aliah. In the past he had shown her and her guards round the markets a few times so Aliah was sure he must have recognised her. Her heart was pounding in her chest, and her palms sweated so much she nearly let go of the goat she was leading.

'Maybe, miss, if you get some time later, you could perhaps do me the honour of breaking your fast with me.' He practically leered at Aliah, and she took a step back.

Fortunately Walter stepped between them. 'It would

not be appropriate for my daughter to eat alone with a man not of our family, sir, as she is recently betrothed.' He grabbed Aliah's arm and pulled her forward before the market manager could respond.

Aliah let out a sigh of relief. 'I thought he recognised me,' she laughed.

'Nay, lass, that one is known for latching onto any new pretty face, and many have taken him up thinking they will get a better spot if they accept his affections. Many have been proved wrong.' Farmer Nobb frowned as he stopped his wagon in the assigned spot. 'It is a good thing you will be leaving after we set up today as he will no doubt not have been put off and we will see him later looking to get you alone. And I really would not like to offend him if I do not have to.'

They helped the farmer set up his stall and put out his vegetables, fruit, cheeses, and eggs for sale. Seamus and Aliah took the goats and oxen to the common to graze. Once they were done the oxen were left with a boy for a copper coin, and the goats taken back to a pen the farmer had set up in their absence.

'We are done now, you can be about your sight seeing,' Farmer Nobb told them. 'I would take some time to break fast at the Horse and Buckle before going too far,' he added, rather loudly.

With that, the farmer went to serve his first customer for the day. His wife shooed them away with her hands. Aliah could not go without saying good-bye, and impulsively hugged the older woman, whispering in her ear, 'Thank you, I shall not forget your help.'

The other woman looked startled, then blushed and

BEGINNINGS

said, 'Be away with you now!'

Walter set off at a purposeful pace, followed by Seamus then Aliah, who was dragging behind and looking back at the stall.

'What about Pauley?' she asked as she realised he was not following.

'It would not be fair to take him where we are going, it is too dangerous. He will go home with the farmer and his wife. They will get him safely back to his parents,' Walter muttered so he could not be over-heard.

Aliah half-turned to go back. 'But we did not get to say good-bye.'

Seamus grabbed her arm before she could head back to the farmer's stand. 'It would look too strange for people looking around Bannock for a few candle-marks to make too much of a farewell,' he said. 'Do not put us in more danger than we already face by doing something people will notice.'

Aliah paused, ready to fight, then realised he was right. She followed behind her two companions feeling a little sad inside that she had not properly thanked and farewelled the young boy, and worried that once again her instincts had nearly gotten them into trouble. If this was what adventuring was like she was not sure it was really the life for her. If she could take back all those times she had wished life had been more exciting when she had been tucked safely behind the castle walls, she would. Now she would be inclined to wish for something very different.

They arrived at the tavern and the smell of bacon cooking as she entered had Aliah's stomach grumbling, reminding her of just how hungry she was. The room was packed and there did not seem to be room for them to sit. Finally, a man made some room for them at a table by the bar. Seamus and Aliah sat while Walter went up to the counter to order them some weak ale and breakfast. Food ordered, he sat down by the man who had made space for them.

'Here for the market?' the man asked, conversationally.

'Helping out my brother,' Walter said. 'He does not need us until packing up time so we are having a look around. My children's first time in Bannock.' Walter looked at them and then took a swig of ale as he waited for their food to arrive.

In the following silence Aliah wondered why they were wasting time in the inn rather than heading straight for the castle. Yes, they were all hungry, but once inside the castle her father could have food bought for them. Her focus drifted as Walter and the townsman continued talking. Finally, a girl brought their food over and she began eating.

As she ate, she noticed a young man by the fire watching them. She went to say something to Walter, but held back because her gut had not been particularly helpful lately. What would it hurt to say something? She was just about to speak when the man who had made room for them at his table stood up. 'If you want to see that view of the castle I was talking about,' he said, 'I have a few errands to run but will be by the common in about half a candle.'

'Thank you. We will consider your offer,' Walter responded, shaking the man's hand.

As he departed the serving girl came over to refill their

tankards with more watered ale. It was not until they continued eating that Aliah remembered the man who had taken an interest in their group. However, when she looked back over by the fire he was gone. *Should I say anything? No, I will just keep and eye out for him.* She finished her meal as fast as she could, wanting to be on her way.

'I am ready to leave now,' she quietly announced when she had finished, dismayed to see that Seamus and Walter had barely touched their food.

'What's your rush?' Walter responded heartily. 'Bannock will still be there after breakfast.' More quietly so only she could hear he said, 'We do not have to be at the common for a while yet and I would rather mark the time here than in such an exposed place as the market where someone could easily recognise you.'

Aliah blinked, and then what was happening dawned on her. They had come to the tavern to meet their guide, and he would wait for them by the green. *I really must pay more attention to what is going on.* She slowly drank her watered-down ale to while away the time as Walter and Seamus finished eating.

'Now I am refreshed, we can look around the market and town,' Walter said, heartily, as he rose. Seamus and Aliah followed suit. Their place at the table was swiftly filled by waiting customers as they left the crowded tavern for the hustle and bustle of the market, which was now in full swing.

The three of them meandered through the stalls looking at goods, but buying nothing. As they neared the green Aliah could see the man from their table looking at some livestock and carrying some parcels. As she went to tell Walter her eye caught a figure casually leaning against a stall. As their friend moved, so did the man. 'So he was not watching us.' Aliah was relieved. At that moment Walter caught sight of their guide and raised his arm to call out. Aliah quickly grabbed his arm and spun him towards the stall. 'Father, look at this!' she gushed, and as they bent towards the cloth she had picked up she whispered, 'I spotted a man interested in our group in the tavern, he is following your friend, I think.' She moved so her back was to the man and said, 'That man behind me with the blue shirt and his hat pulled down low.'

'It is truly lovely, daughter, but I do not think we can afford the price. We will go and look at a stall more suited to us.' Seamus was frowning as he had seen their guide and did not understand why they were heading off in the opposite direction. They finally stopped by a pastry stall where Walter bought a pastry. He paid a little extra to have the baker's boy deliver it, with the message, 'Your companions will wait for you in the stable, but do not bring your friend.'

As they walked back to the tavern through the market, Aliah asked, 'Will he understand the message?'

'I understood it, and I am guessing I have not been at this as long as he has.' Seamus laughed. 'Good on you for spotting he was being followed. You have saved us from a bit of bother.'

'You are right, son, he has been doing this for some time. In fact, he and I met in the castle here. He helped me when I needed eyes and ears to get out of a difficult situation.'

They were heading through the back streets towards

the tavern, mingling with the crowd, when Walter suddenly stopped. There was a figure dressed all in black standing outside the gate to the tavern's back yard. As he moved to talk to one of the men with him, Aliah glimpsed the flash of a gold lightening bolt. *Oh no. A Gold Wizard,* she thought. At that moment the wizard seemed to look over the crowd and stare straight at Walter.

'Carry on walking,' Walter whispered. 'Stay in the markets and meet me back here in a candle-mark.'

Then he was off, running back through the crowd. The wizard shouted and he began running towards them followed by two soldiers. Aliah grabbed Seamus' hand to steal her nerves and tried to do what everyone else was doing, watching the three running men chase after another. She let out her breath as they ran straight past her and Seamus without even a glance.

The ruckus over, people continued on with their business. Aliah let go of Seamus' hand and they walked past the tavern back into the market. Sick to the stomach, she tried to show interest in shopping. Seamus even used some of his hard earned coin to buy a knife and a leather sheath. 'Just in case,' he whispered to her. And it was then she realised that their weapons were still with the farmer.

'Should we go back and get ours?' she asked him.

'I am pretty sure that would not be a good idea. Would you like a knife? I could get you one too?' Aliah shook her head. She was not sure she could use one effectively in close combat.

'If we have trouble I will just have to try your new form of unarmed combat.' Her eyes were twinkling as she looked at him.

The candle-mark seemed to drag, but finally the church bell tolled and they headed back to the inn to meet with Walter. Aliah pulled Seamus to a stop. The man leaning against the wall of the alley beside the tavern was the same man who had been watching their guide earlier. 'Keep walking,' she told Seamus.

'What now?' he asked as she stopped by a stall to look.

'See that man over there?'

Seamus nodded.

'He is the one who was watching our guide.'

The man was carefully searching the crowd around him.

'What do you want to do? Do you want me to cause a diversion and you can go in?'

Aliah felt a rush of warmth that he was prepared to risk himself to get her into the castle. Although she knew it would be the simplest solution, it did not feel right. She walked around the stall picking up necklaces and putting them down, watching both the man by the inn and Seamus. She could not read from his face what he wanted her to do.

'I know another way into the castle grounds. It is similar to the one I think Walter wanted us to take from the inn. We could try that way. But it would mean we would have to go it alone. What do you think?' Aliah deliberately looked at the necklace she was holding rather than his face, as she did not want to see his reaction. She could tell he was watching her, and probably chewing his lip while he decided what to answer.

'I think that may be a better option,' he finally said. He reached over to pay the stallholder for the necklace Aliah held. 'To divert suspicion,' he whispered. 'That will do nicely for our mother.'

'I am sure she will love it,' the woman said as she passed his parcel over to him.

They slowly wandered through the market again, making sure that the man from outside the tavern was not following them. Seamus added a leather bag to his purchases for the day, and swiftly stowed his two parcels in it. When they were satisfied they were not being followed, Aliah led them through the streets near the wall to another tavern.

'I am beginning to see a pattern here.' Seamus laughed.

'It seems one of my ancestors liked to nip out for a drink or two.' Aliah shared the family joke with him, relieving a bit of the tension she felt.

There was no one hanging round outside this tavern, so Aliah decided it was quite safe going down the alleyway to the door leading to the back yard. Her hand stopped on the door handle as the sound of feet running towards them reached her ears. She hardly knew what was happening as a weight bowled into her. She and Seamus fell through the door with a stranger on top of them.

Seamus was up first, knife drawn, and hauling the other person to their feet.

'Shut the gate, you fool. They will know where I have gone.'

Seamus did not move. His knife was held at the man's throat. The man shook his head and managed to wiggle his foot and lift it to shut the gate. He stared at Seamus, who glared back at him. A few moments later there were running feet in the alleyway and the man visibly relaxed.

'That was lucky finding you here.' His dark blue eyes

twinkled as he smiled at Seamus and Aliah.

Seamus glowered back as Aliah picked herself up off the ground, brushing herself off and checking for wounds. She noticed a bundle on the ground and looked at the man Seamus held. They had helped a common thief. She shook her head in disgust.

'Let him go, Seamus. No doubt the people he stole this from will find him soon enough. If they don't, the city guard will.'

'You think I stole that.' The man burst out laughing. Not really the response Aliah was expecting. Even Seamus looked perplexed.

'You do not recognise me? My disguises must be getting better.' The man was almost doubled over in laughter.

'Your Highness.' The man bowed to Aliah. 'I am at your service.'

'And you are also sometimes called your Highness, but as we are in Aria, I will stick to sir.' He bowed to Seamus as much as he could with a knife held to his throat, giving Aliah an even bigger surprise. 'I have been at your father's court a number of times and I never forget a face, even when it is such a long way from home.'

'I am Dominic Du Bray, son of the Count of Du Bray, or the Eastern Duchy as it is now called, and your father's top information gatherer.' He looked down at the knife. 'Now that we have been introduced we can dispense with that.'

Aliah shook her head and Seamus did not move. If this man worked for her father then his first allegiance was to him. If he left orders for his daughter to be brought back to the court then he would do just that, publicly, and their plan would be for nothing.

BEGINNINGS

Dominic watched Aliah's face and knew that his situation had not changed. 'You look worried, my princess.'

'I think I know what it is,' Seamus answered for her. 'You work for her father, and we are trying to sneak in to see her father. So you do not exactly fit in with our plans.'

'And if you do work for my father surely you are meant to pick me up and carry me publicly back to court. If you do not do this, then you are not working for my father but another group and then, sir, I am not sure I trust you.'

Dominic laughed. 'You definitely have your father's brains and your mother's beauty. An interesting mix! Let me quickly explain. I am a spy, and as such I get a very broad interpretation of what is in the best interests of the kingdom, being as I cannot always get word to your father or my master to clarify every detail.

'In this instance, I have been working with Walter to return you to your father, which is exactly what he commanded me do should I come across you. I am just choosing to do that in a very secret way.

'In addition, I have become aware there are some men close to your father who do not have his or the kingdom's best interests at heart. I have been investigating them and that is why I am followed, and we had trouble today. Does that explain this rather strange situation to your satisfaction?'

Aliah frowned, and looked at Seamus. He shrugged his shoulders, seeming to say it was her call.

Dominic interrupted. 'We need to move. The king has a council until noon, and the easiest way for me to get his attention without others being present is when he is with them. He can leave the room as required and those others we want to avoid can be asked to remain and continue with state business.'

'Don't we need to wait for Walter?' Seamus asked.

'Walter is otherwise detained at the moment. We can do nothing for him until we get to the king.'

Aliah looked at Seamus and he nodded. 'I cannot say I trust you,' Aliah said, 'But at this moment I cannot let you go either. I think it best if we all travel together until I make up my mind.'

'Well isn't that just a vote of confidence!' Dominic laughed. 'We had best be moving then,' he said as he picked up the packages off the ground and led them into the kitchen of the inn.

The room bustled with activity. The cook and her boy were still making breakfast for the crowded tavern, and serving girls were coming in and out. They did not appear to even see Dominic leading them through their domain and into the storeroom. Noticing Seamus and Aliah's curious glances, Dominic advised them that the tavern was paid handsomely by the crown not to see such things as strange people passing through. Dominic closed the storeroom door behind them and in the gloomy light of the room's one window he handed Aliah one of the bundles he had picked up off the ground, the other he gave to Seamus.

'You will probably be needing these,' he told them. They unwrapped the parcels to find they contained the weapons they had left with the farmer and his wife. 'The way we are going is quite safe, but it is always better to be sure than dead.' And with that, he pulled a dresser out from beneath the window, revealing a door. He opened the door and gestured for them to go through.

Aliah went first with Seamus following. Coming last, Dominic closed the door then pulled a cord that ran through the door, bringing the chest back into place. He squeezed past Aliah and Seamus until he had the lead. They waited a moment until their eyes adjusted to the darkness, then began moving.

'Right then, we head down first, walk for about half a candle-mark, then we go up. In the downwards and upwards sections it will be best not to talk as going down we are near the tavern and could be over-heard, and the same applies when going up as we are in the castle grounds. The rest of the way is under the streets of the city, and you would have to be very loud for anyone to hear us.'

He led them down some stairs, and as they walked they could hear the noise from the tavern. When it was silent, and they had been walking on the flat for some time, Aliah chanced conversation. 'You seem to know these tunnels well.'

'Although they were designed as escape routes for the royal family, there are others of us who need to come and go in secret who also use them,' Dominic answered.

'So these are considered spy-ways?' Aliah asked.

'Spy is such and ugly word, don't you think? Let us just say that a king needs information and sometimes that information needs to be gathered in secret. There are those of us with certain skills who find this occupation the best way to serve our king and the kingdom. We are merely soldiers with different skills. And sometimes we need to come and go without others knowing, so we use these secret passages.' Aliah could hear the smile in his answer.

'But I find this an unusual occupation for you. Surely your father, the duke, does not think this is a suitable way for you to spend your time. He is not a strong supporter of the crown. Some would perhaps say he is even an enemy.'

'And you would be right, my princess. As one of the few surviving Duchies from pre-Natari times my family considers your father to be a foreign king imposed on us as our liege lord.'

'And you do not?' Seamus asked.

'No. But maybe that is because I am a second son and will not inherit my father's title. I also have not inherited his commitment to our historic past. I am more interested in maintaining a prosperous Aria, and I also admire the king's stance on men being rewarded on merit, rather than title. And while the nation continues to thrive under his stewardship he will have my full support.'

'Besides, my father thinks I am spending my time at court looking for a suitably rich bride to marry. For him, that is exactly the thing a second son should do.'

'Oh.' Aliah could not think of anything to say to that. This man was not what she had expected. Neither when she had first met him, nor when she found out he was a spy in her father's employ. For some reason she had always believed spies were a little unscrupulous, without honour, little better than thieves. But Dominic did not seem to fit easily into the image she had. That was if he was to be trusted, and only time would tell that.

They walked in silence and it seemed like no time at all before they found themselves walking up hill. *The castle already,* Aliah thought, and immediately butterflies invaded her stomach. She was a little scared about seeing her father again, and also about being caught in the castle. The butterflies flew faster as they reached the stairs and began their ascent.

Dominic pushed open a door, and they found themselves in the castle laundry. The women did not stop their work as Dominic led his companions through the laundry to a locked room at the end. Producing a key, he opened the door and hustled them in. Inside the room was an array of clothes and a screened off section.

'I think you will find a tub of water behind that screen,' Dominic said to Aliah. 'Wash up quickly and put up your hair. There is a servant's uniform and scarf for your head. Change as quickly as you can.'

'You seem well prepared,' Aliah said.

'Different tunnel, same plan as I had with Walter,' Dominic replied. 'Now hurry, we have not got much time before the noon bell.' It was only then Aliah realised he was the same man they had eaten breakfast with.

Aliah washed as quickly as she could, wishing she had time to actually soak in the bath rather than just rinse the grime of travel off herself. And oh, to have the time to wash her hair! That would be a luxury.

She emerged to find her companions dressed in palace livery, taking turns in front of a mirror to shave off their travel growth so they would not stand out amongst the clean-shaven staff. As he stopped what he was doing to see she was fit to be presented, Aliah realised Dominic was not as old as she first thought. Clean-shaven and freshly washed with his hair tied back in the customary ponytail of courtiers, he looked to be only a little older than Seamus.

He handed Aliah an apron to put over her skirts and she realised he was laughing at her, 'Ah, now you can see me as the son of a duke rather than a slimy spy.' His blue eyes twinkled for a moment, then his face changed and he was all business again.

'Right, Seamus, you can carry that sword as the princess cannot be carrying that as a servant. Hold it as though you are going to present it to the king. Put your knives in that bag you have and carry it over your shoulder. All of them! We will need to leave them all at the door though, as to go into the presence of the king armed invites certain death.'

'They are all in there. It is the same custom in my father's court. I know the penalty of baring arms in the king's presence,' Seamus told him looking very serious.

'Ah, we are ready then. Come!' Dominic put his hands on his hips, faced them and gave them a good once over to ensure they would fit in. 'You cannot take those packs with you, though. Place them under the bench there and we will come back and get them later.' They placed their travelling packs under the bench and followed Dominic out through the laundry, across the courtyard, and into the kitchens. There he found a tray with a pitcher of water and a bowl of fruit, which had conveniently been prepared for someone. The under-cook, who was about to add some flowers to the tray, was about to complain

BEGINNINGS

when he realised it was Dominic doing the stealing. He stopped mid-word and reached for a new tray as if that had been his intention all along. Dominic waved and led his team to the back stairway used by the palace servants.

They followed him up three flights of winding stairs barely two people wide. Her jaunts around the castle using the servants' staircases told Aliah they were going to her father's personal suite. As they entered the corridor she nearly bumped into Dominic, who had stopped short. Aliah just caught a glimpse of a black robe as she ducked her head, hoping not to be seen. She need not have feared because Gaius would never take a second look at an actual servant.

'Dominic.' He sneered. 'Still playing at spies. Haven't you found a real job yet?'

'Gaius. Such a pleasure to see you, as always. I would have thought guarding prisoners was beneath you now you have been raised to The Silver.'

Aliah could hear the sneer in Gaius' voice. 'This is a criminal we have been looking for for some time. As the only wizard with enough power to contain him should he attack, I have the responsibility of taking him to Millard for questioning.'

'Mmm, I was under the impression the king had asked to see this particular criminal immediately on his capture.' Dominic casually leaned against the wall and Aliah caught a glimpse of Walter behind Gaius. She could not be sure, but it looked as though he winked. 'I am heading to the king now, why don't you let me take him off your hands? Save you the trouble.'

Trapped, Gaius faltered before he answered. 'I will

take him. I could not trust him in your care.' He stopped and sniffed. 'I can smell her. The princess.' He sniffed again. 'She was on Walton, and I smell her stronger now.'

Aliah tensed, and almost ran. It curdled her stomach when Gaius used his sensing ability.

'Gaius, I feel you are really losing it. Perhaps it is the pressure of being elevated to the silver so early. The princess? On Walton? Really? You imagine her everywhere. And of course you can smell her here. How many times has she been in these halls? Maybe I should talk to Millard about giving you a break. We cannot have you cracking up completely.'

Gaius stiffened at the veiled insult to his skills. 'Let us get this prisoner to the king. Then I can be rid of your loathsome presence.'

Dominic followed Gaius and Walter back to the door of the king's personal chambers. They were stopped outside by one of his personal guard.

'Your business?' the older of the two guards barked.

'I have fresh water and fruit for the king's rooms, as he requested. His new sword has arrived, and I have an urgent message to be delivered to him,' Dominic responded. 'Oh,' he said as if he only just remembered. 'And after I am done I believe Gaius would like to see him. He has a rather important prisoner I believe the king is most keen to see before anyone else.'

'The king is in council.' The guard stood stony faced.

'The message cannot wait,' Dominic persisted. 'It is an urgent matter from the Fox.'

The guard's face barely changed. 'Broad,' he said to the younger guard. 'Tell the king he has a message from the

BEGINNINGS

Fox. Discretely, mind you. You can take the refreshments into the king's room and wait there, but the sword stays out here.'

'Surely you cannot expect me to wait while he goes first.' Gaius spluttered.

Stoney faced the Guard responded, 'The Fox always takes precedence.'

Dominic indicated the bench against the far wall and Seamus placed the sword and his bag of knives there, taking care not to let Gaius get a good look at his face. Aliah then followed him and Dominic into her father's personal sitting room. The guard closed the door firmly behind them. Seamus and Aliah stood together by the window while Dominic made himself comfortable in a chair by the fire. The very chair Aliah had sat in when her father told her she was to leave home.

It was odd being back in her father's outer-chamber under such different circumstances. She was not the trusting girl who had left this room more than two moon turns ago. Then, she had thought her father was infallible. She now knew he was just as able to fall prey to bad advice as any other man. There was a noise outside and her stomach clenched. Seamus took her hand, sensing her unease, and gave it a quick squeeze before dropping it as the door opened.

14
AN AUDIENCE
WITH THE KING

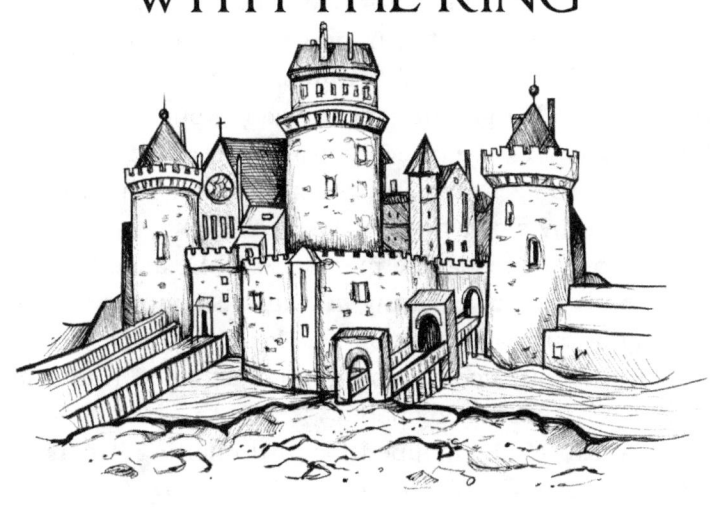

'Dominic, please tell me that is not who I think it is standing out there with Gaius. I was under the impression we had agreed he was to be left in peace until we uncovered what is really going on with the wizard council?' The tall, lean, dark haired man scolded as he took the gold coronet off his head and placed it on a stand on the chest beside the door. 'And please, if you can, be quick with your report. I have a squabbling council who cannot decide what they want me to do about a rather large fleet of ships heading our way. They not only need guidance to make the right decision, but also to stop them throttling each other. Actually, I need someone to stop me from throttling all of them.'

'Your Majesty, it *is* who you think outside the door, and all will become clear soon,' Dominic said as he bowed to his king, and at the same time glanced towards the window.

The king stopped mid-stride, frowning. 'Do you not bow in the presence of your monarch?' His haughty blue eyes glared at Aliah and Seamus. Seamus inclined his head, a suitable greeting for the son of one monarch to his superior. This earned him a frown and there were obviously some harsh words on the way, which Aliah forestalled by stepping forward.

'Do you not recognise me, father?' she asked as she removed the cloth covering her hair. Seamus was sure it was not often King Terion was lost for words, but the sudden appearance of his daughter stopped him mid-sentence, mouth wide open.

'Aliahanna?' he stepped forward opening his arms. 'You are safe? Thank the goddess!'

Aliah ran to her father and entered his warm embrace. Seamus knew the moment the king took over from the father by the change in expression on the face over Aliah's shoulder. The king pushed his daughter away to arms length. 'Where have you been? Do you know how much trouble you have caused? We are on the brink of war and your behaviour may or may not have had a little something to do with that, depending on who I speak to. Do you know how worried I have been?'

BEGINNINGS

'If I may, sire?' Dominic stepped forward. 'Time is of the essence here. Perhaps you should hear the princesses' story, then maybe ask questions after?' There was a long pause before the king nodded his assent, and led Aliah over to the fire. Dominic gave up his chair for the princess, coming to stand by the window beside Seamus.

The king and his daughter talked in low voices for some time with Seamus and Dominic watching on. By the time they finished Seamus was stiff and tired and grumpy.

'So, young man, it seems I have you, among others, to thank for looking after my daughter.' The king finally turned and looked at Seamus. 'While I appreciate what you have done for my family I cannot abide bad manners. I will ask you again to bow in the presence of your king. Did your family not teach you manners?'

Seamus raised an eyebrow at Aliah, and she smiled back at him. Obviously she had told her story, but not all of his. It was up to him to tell the king who he was if he chose. 'Apologies, sir, I did not mean to offend, but as my father is my king, I bow to none but him. And while I do not wish to appear rude, well, it is awkward.'

The king laughed. 'Well, I thought I could be shocked no more today, but it looks like I was wrong. No one would have bet my daughter would stumble on the errant son of the Duke of Hand. Need I remind you, young Seamus, in this court you are considered one of my subjects not the son of a Monarch, but I understand your sentiments and will forego formalities today only.'

Seamus bowed his head in acknowledgment of the courtesy the king had just granted him. This was not an issue to push at the moment, they all had far more to worry about than the strained relations between Hand and the crown.

'And you, lad, what do you make of my daughter's tale? That Spearon never intended to wed her and bind our countries, but always intended to invade us?' King Terion asked his spy.

'Sire.' Dominic stepped forward. 'It does tie in with what I have been hearing on my travels. There is a captain in Port Marden who saw a fleet massing before the princess could even make land there. I heard talk in the taverns there that the sailors on the princesses' ship were not that concerned about losing their lord's prospective bride as it seems he was not in a mood to marry her anyway. There were many hints about how the princess would be used, though. And none of them sounded like fun.'

The king's brow furrowed. 'And I guess you have your friend out there because you give some credence to his ramblings about a plot to de-stabilise my rule and for the wizard's council to take over running Aria?'

'I may not agree with all he says as I have not been able to verify it all. I have, however, spoken to enough people to know the captain on your daughter's boat was working with some people high up in your government here, and it was they who were pushing for the princess to be found, not the captain himself. There have also been wizards around the countryside stirring unrest, trying to find the princess. They have been working independently of your guard, hand in hand with mercenaries. You have to ask why?'

'So you believe there is a plot?' The king asked point blank.

BEGINNINGS

'I believe something is going on. I also know that Walton has been working on uncovering this for a lot longer than I, and it might benefit you to talk with him and find out what he knows.'

The king pondered for a time. 'He has been discredited by both my council and the Council of Wizards. I would lose a lot of support if it were found I had met with him behind their backs, and it is something Gaius would not keep to himself.'

Aliah placed her hand on her father's arm. 'Perhaps you could have one of your guards take Walter ... Walton to the dungeons, thank Gaius and dismiss him, then have Walton brought back. He did risk his life to bring me home, and I believe he deserves a hearing.'

There was a further silence, and the king sighed. 'Dominic, you and I will speak with him. Aliah, put your head covering back on and I will have the guards take you to my private study. They will have some food brought for you and the young man. We will meet there after we have talked.'

'But ... this has nothing to do with me anymore.' Seamus stepped forward, 'I would like to leave.' He had had enough of all this intrigue. His part was done and all he wanted now was to find out who Walter would have him go to for training and be on his way.

The king held up his hand. 'I am sorry, young man, but this is the business of my realm we discuss, and I make the decisions on what is important and what can wait. This meeting is the most important thing at the moment, your future can wait. We will not decide anything about you without your presence. Rest assured. In the

237

meantime, please enjoy my hospitality.'

Seamus looked at Aliah, she shrugged her shoulders. Reluctantly, Seamus agreed and followed the guard down the corridor to the king's study.

'I have done my bit, I just want to be away from here.' Seamus paced around the study once the door was closed.

'Be fair, Seamus.' Aliah leaned against her father's desk. 'We have done our job but we may still be needed to help Aria survive this war. We may still have important information they need. We may even have a role to play. We should wait and hear what comes out of this meeting. Walter and Dominic know way more than they told us, and it is only right my father hears their council. This could be their only chance to get their point across without my father's advisors being present.'

'I know all that, but I do not know what I can contribute now. All I want is for Walter to keep his end of the bargain and send me on to someone who can help me manage my magic.' Seamus slumped in a chair in front of the desk.

'I know that is what you want.' Aliah frowned at him, 'But can you really desert Aria in her time of need? This will affect the people of the Southern Duchies as well.'

Seamus frowned and reluctantly had to admit he probably would not. Then, before he could find something else to grumble about, the soldier who had escorted them brought in a tray of bread and cheese and a pitcher of fresh, cold milk. There were also a few small honey cakes. Aliah thanked him, and the two fell on the food like they had not eaten in days. As they ate, Seamus realised some of his bad mood was due to hunger. He was so much happier once his stomach was full.

BEGINNINGS

When they finished, Aliah challenged him to a game of Last Man using the board and pieces her father had set up in the corner. The strategy of the war game had him enthralled for a time, but after he won one game and Aliah another, he began to get bored and started pacing the room again.

'Aliah? Do you think your father has a book on the prophecy we have been hearing so much about? I do not believe I have ever seen it. We have time we may as well have a look at it.' Seamus did not know why the idea popped into his head.

'I think so.' Aliah went to a shelf over the other side of the room, and after a few minutes she took down a book. Taking it over to her father's desk she opened it up and began flipping through it. 'Here it is!' She pointed to a page and Seamus went over to read.

'It is from a seer who made the prophecy during the Natari expansion, apparently. She was in Hand at the time.'

Seamus looked where her finger pointed.

'When the new power rises
And the Wizard and Warrior meet,
Old and new blood will combine
To save one and all.'

'That is really vague!' Seamus was a little disappointed. 'It could mean anyone or in any time. Is there anything else?'

'Not here, although there might be in the main castle library. This could be real or it could just be propaganda to try and unite the two nations,' Aliah suggested as she put the book back. 'This was written just after the Natari invasion after all.'

239

Seamus nodded thoughtfully. 'It did not do a very good job if that was the intention. I wonder if my people have a similar prophecy? If we did, then maybe it might actually mean something.'

Seamus continued his pacing and Aliah went back to the game of Last Man she was playing against herself. Sunset was near when the door finally opened and the king entered along with Dominic, Walter, and another man about the age of Aliah's father dressed in guard's livery. Seamus started at the sight of a military man, but Aliah beamed. 'Uncle Tomas. Seamus, this is father's oldest friend and captain of his personal guard.'

'Aliah, you have led us on a fine chase. My boys have had bets on how long it would take me to find you, but young Shane won. He said I wouldn't. You would find us when you were ready.' He returned Aliah's smile.

'I am sorry to cut this short,' King Terion interrupted. 'But, Tomas, you cannot tell Shane or anyone that Aliah came back. All must think her still lost for our plans to work.'

'Yes, yes, of course,' Tomas looked abashed.

'Plans?' Seamus stepped forward. 'I hope they do not include me?'

'Yes, they do include you, in so far as you want to be included.' The king firmly held is gaze. 'I make no apologies about that. Aria faces a war and there are things to take into consideration that you are not party to. However, we have not set anything in stone with regards to your participation. What you do from here is up to you. Of course we hope you take a certain path but I will not force you. Look what happened when I did that with

240

BEGINNINGS

Aliah. I will not make that same mistake again.'

Aliah stepped forward. 'Does that mean I can come home father?'

King Terion hugged his daughter. 'No, my sweet, I am sorry. If there is one thing I am convinced of it is you are not safe around me and you must remain lost. How you remain lost though will be up to you.'

The king released his daughter and went and sat behind his desk. He gestured for the others to sit in the various chairs around the room, with Aliah and Seamus taking the two seats in front of him.

'After much discussion I have become open to the possibility that not all of my council—or those on the wizards' council—have our people's best interests at heart. The depth of this, I have no way of knowing, but I feel the only way to find out is to carry on as if this visit never occurred, at least in the open. I plan to have a few select people closely watched by some of Dominic's friends, and we will wait and see if they slip up.'

'In the meantime I need to get ready for a war that we are ill prepared to fight. One of the things we were discussing today was sending an envoy to the Isle of Hand and suggesting we join forces to defend the South. Many in my council, some of whom I now suspect to be sabotaging plans for our defence, talked the council out of that idea. I would like to do that anyway, sending you as secret envoys.' King Terion looked directly at Seamus.

'But, I cannot go back,' Seamus said. 'Even if I wanted to.'

'Ah, yes. Your reason for leaving. Walter told me you could become a wizard of great strength one day with the proper training. I can only imagine what that means within your family. By now they must have guessed the reason you ran away, and this will make it difficult when you see them again.'

'They may have guessed,' Seamus admitted. 'If they have, then I will not be welcomed back into the family.' Seamus hung his head, there was no point in wishing for something that would never happen.

'You might be surprised.' The king reached into a drawer in his desk and pulled out a letter, which he handed to Seamus. 'Go ahead, read it.'

Seamus looked at the letter. The writing seemed familiar. As he read he realised it was from his mother to the king. She wrote she had reason to believe her son was travelling to the Wizard Isles and she would appreciate the king letting her know when he arrived. If he could also pass on whether he was in good health, and let him know his mother would not be against receiving an occasional letter.

A great wave of homesickness rolled through Seamus, then he realised the reality. 'My father will never accept me back.'

'No. Perhaps not. But you will be going to the Isle of Hand as my representative and therefore under my protection. I just wanted you to know that should you return, you would have at least one supporter in your father's court. Think on it.'

'And if I choose not to return?'

'You could be admitted to the school on the Isle of Wizards to learn magic. Or if you choose not to learn magic there, then Walter says he found a mage in Nataria who would consider taking you on as an apprentice.'

BEGINNINGS

'He is a good person and a good teacher.' Walter said encouragingly. Seamus frowned, unsure of what to do.

'Of course, if you decide to become my envoy then Walter could travel with you as an advisor and you could continue your magic training under his care. Walter has agreed to this.' The king's eyebrows raised questioningly.

Seamus frowned and gnawed his lip. Unsure what to do, he was saved from answering by Aliah.

'And what about me? What are my options?'

'There are two I can see to keep you safe.' Her father's attention swung to her. 'Tomas has offered to escort you to his estates and there you will be protected by his wife and his son, Angus, who you know runs the estate in his father's absence.'

'No offence, Tomas, but your home is in the Highlands, surrounded by forests and mountains on all sides. And Angus and I have never gotten on. We would drive Alyssa mad with our fighting.'

Tomas laughed. 'But you would be safe, and Alyssa would enjoy some female company after raising four boys.'

'And the other option?' Aliah dismissed this one immediately and looked at her father to see if he could do better with his alternative.

'The other option would be to spend some time with my cousin in the Natari Capital. He is a minor noble as things go in the Empire, but he could introduce you to court and you could perhaps find a suitable match there.'

Seamus held his breath for the explosion, and was not disappointed by its magnitude even if Aliah's voice was controlled and low.

'So, you failed to marry me off to some barbarian who

really did not want to marry me, and then you tell me my only other options to stay safe are to hide in the middle of nowhere, or to marry some foreigner. Meanwhile Seamus gets to be an envoy or learn magic, or both. That is the only role you see for me in your narrow view?' The room was quiet, as if no one was sure how to treat this outburst. Before anyone could speak Aliah continued. 'Well, I am just as capable of being an envoy to the Isle of Hand as Seamus! I am as educated and as able to hold my own in a court. Once more, I would be out of sight of the court here while you ferreted out your enemies.' She sat back and folded her arms.

Dominic burst out laughing, which served to anger Aliah even more. 'Sire, she has you there. And in this instance two envoys may be better than one!'

'I don't need your support,' Aliah flung at him.

Dominic's face remained impassive as the king responded. 'Well, I see nothing wrong with both of you going as my envoys. And you, Dominic, can accompany them to ensure my needs are met, as a guard of course, so you are not noticed. Walter you can be their trusted advisor and tutor. Tomas, you can send your son, Daniel, and a couple of men as honour guards. I am sure your second son can keep these two in line.'

And with that, it was all organised, much to Seamus' annoyance. He was of course, going to choose to be the king's envoy as he wanted to be a part of the fight to save his country, and the fact Walter would continue to teach him was a big bonus. But to have the decision taken away was most frustrating.

While Seamus fumed and went over what he wanted

to say in his head, the king began drawing up requisitions, orders, and formal letters of introduction. The others chatted quietly. As Seamus went to speak there was a knock on the door.

'Sire. Chief Advisor Millard is requesting an audience,' the guard announced.

'Where is he?' the king asked.

'He is standing outside, sire. He knows you have Captain Tomas and someone else in here.'

The king was silent for a moment. 'Dominic, take Walter and my daughter the back way to the docks. The Golden Hawk is ready to sail on my order. Seamus and his guard will join you soon.' He handed Dominic some papers. 'You can get suitable supplies at Port Isby. Seamus will have the official letters of introduction when he boards.' The king's voice was low so it would not carry.

Dominic did not delay. Leading the others to the chest by the Last Man table, he fiddled around for something and the chest moved into the room revealing a hidden passage. When they were safely inside and the chest had swung silently back in place, the king nodded to the guard. A man in wizard's robes barged into the room seconds after the guard had opened the door.

'Forgive my intrusion, sire.' He bowed. 'You had not returned and the council has disbanded, then Gaius informed me we had captured Walton and that you were in private meetings. I thought you might need my services, so I stayed behind.'

'Ahh, Millard, how helpful you are. However, this is nothing you can assist with.'

'You look to be writing, sire, may I at least scribe for you?'

'That will not be necessary, it is only a short personal note. Wizard Millard, meet Seamus, Heir to the Duke of Hand. He has been missing for some time on a personal journey of discovery. One of Tomas' men found him in the city today and brought him here knowing his mother had asked me to look out for his safety. He is about to depart for home on the Golden Hawk, which should be passing by the Isle in its reconnaissance mission.' The king handed Seamus the letter he had just added his seal to, plus two others. 'This is for your mother, the other two are for your father. Tomas, see to it that trunk waiting in my room is sent with him. It contains gifts for the duke and duchess. And, if you could spare Daniel and a couple of guards to go with Seamus to ensure he makes it to the Golden Hawk, I would appreciate it, as would his mother I think.'

'Your Highness.' Tomas bowed and left the room.

'So this is the young man who has been leading his family on a merry dance?' Wizard Millard's smile seemed overly friendly and Seamus felt a whisper as the other wizard tried to sense his magic. 'And the rumours he is a magic user are untrue?'

Seamus froze, surely a wizard of the gold could feel his magic even if it were shielded.

'I guess they were not true if you cannot detect any magic in him,' the king responded. 'Now, young man, I hope you have a pleasant journey, and perhaps next time you will think a little about how your mother will feel when you try to adventure off!' He shook Seamus' hand and called for the guard. 'Please take this young man to my chambers where he is to wait until Guard Daniel arrives to take him to his ship. 'God speed, young man.'

'Now, Millard, perhaps you can inform me of what the council decided in my absence ...' And with that the king moved on to other matters, dismissing Seamus.

In the king's chamber Seamus waited, with the guard firmly on the inside of the door this time as if he did not trust him. A large trunk had been added to the furnishings, and Seamus resisted the urge to open it and see what was inside. Instead, he sat down in a chair and quietly waited for his escort. He used the time to mull over his encounter with Wizard Millard.

He knew his shielding was perfect now. Walter had had him work on it every morning before they slept until he could perform small magics such as creating a light without leaking. That said, Walter told him a stronger wizard could always tell a lesser wizard, even when they were shielded. So that meant one of two things. Either Millard was not truly strong enough to be a gold, or Seamus was stronger in magic than one of the strongest wizards on the wizard council. Then a third option occurred to him. Was Millard playing some sort of twisted game by not admitting to his magic?

It seemed an age before there was a knock at the door and a young guardsman entered. He was obviously Tomas' son, with the same blond wavy hair and laughing brown eyes.

'Your Lordship.' He made a rather sketchy bow. 'I trust you are ready to travel.'

'According to the king, I am.' Seamus grinned, instantly liking the young man. 'Please, call me Seamus. We have a long voyage and to stand on ceremony would be a shame.'

'Yes, that is true. Come now. The captain is rather grumpy at being delayed for so long. Afraid he might miss the tide or something. Then again, he is normally grumpy so it is hard to tell. Boys, I have Lord Seamus, so I guess the trunk is yours,' he said to the two guardsmen standing behind him.'

Protesting, they picked up the trunk between them and carried it out of the castle to the waiting carriage. All four young men jumped aboard and they were soon off to the harbour.

The ship was a large clipper and a hive of activity. The young men left the carriage, and one of the guards called a sailor to take the trunk to Seamus' cabin. They then led Seamus on board, one in front and two behind, just to make sure he did not escape.

The captain stopped them as they boarded. 'Guardsman Cameron, and our final guest for the Isle of Hand, I presume.'

'All present and correct, captain.'

15
A NEW JOURNEY BEGINS

'About blimmin time! We nearly missed the tide because of your tardiness. You share a cabin with Dominic and Walter,' he said to Seamus. 'You gentlemen are across the way. The boy'll show you!'

'Yes, sir!' Daniel performed a mock salute for the captain, who had already moved away as soon as he had spoken to them. After all, he had no time for pleasantries, he had a ship to get underway. As they walked towards the stairs to the cabins Daniel said under his breath,

'And I can see by the fact they are still loading it was only us they were waiting on.' His companions laughed as they followed the boy below deck.

Seamus' cabin door was opened first and he could see a room larger than expected. There were three beds around the walls, and a table bolted to the floor in the middle. Beside the table was the trunk the king had sent, and on top were his and Aliah's packs and the bag with his knives. Through the other door he could see the room for the guards was a mirror image. Daniel and the guards went to settle themselves in and Seamus entered his room to find Dominic had been hidden by the door.

'Here at last,' he said to Seamus. 'Make yourself comfortable. We will not be allowed out until the ship is well underway. Captain Hanks does not like anyone under his feet while he leaves the harbour. A boy will bring us supper, and then I think we should all get a good night's sleep.'

Seamus was about to ask after Walter when the door opened and he entered. He was dressed in smart simple clothes and looked younger than he had before. Seamus guessed this must be what he really looked like and was surprised to see he was around his father's age, maybe a little older. Walter was carrying some reading materials. 'Princess Aliah's trunk is a bit of a mish-mash of things. Some for her and some for us, I suspect this is the same.' He pointed to the trunk that came with Seamus.

'Where is Aliah?' Seamus asked, realising no one had mentioned her since she left the king's study.

Walter shut the door behind him before answering Seamus' question. 'She is in the cabin down the end of the hall. It is usually used for the maids of travelling ladies. It is best no one know who she is until we have left Port Isby. By then no one will be able to tell anyone else she is on board.'

'The captain knows, of course. But he has worked solely under the king's orders since the king gave him his first ship. He is more than trustworthy,' Dominic added.

'Oh.' Seamus answered the same time there was a knock on the door. The ship boy who led them to the cabins entered carrying hot stew and bread for their evening meal. A slightly older boy carrying a pitcher of ale followed him.

After finishing their meal a quick look out the window showed the ship slowly leaving a darkening harbour. Almost as one they decided it was time for sleep and rolled into their beds. Seamus was asleep almost before his head hit the pillow. He had been going for over a day and a half without much rest and even the hard bed could not prevent his body from getting the sleep it craved.

The rocking boat kept Seamus asleep until a knock on the door brought the ships' boy back with food to break their fast. After they had eaten, the three took turns in the confined space at washing and changing into the clothes provided for them by the king. Dominic looked resplendent in his guard's uniform, and Walter very dignified in his black advisor robes. Seamus nearly choked when he saw the splendour the king expected him to prance about in.

'I'm not wearing that! I'll look like one of those court toadies.' He spluttered holding up some sky blue silk trousers and a white ruffled shirt. It did not help that

Walter and Dominic were rolling on their beds laughing at his discomfort.

'The king could hardly send you home in what you are wearing, it would have been a sign of contempt for the duke to see you so. Also, you are entering your father's court as the king's representative, so he would like you to dress appropriately. Your clothes need to display his wealth and power,' Dominic solemnly advised him when he finally calmed down.

Seamus had to admit there was some sense in all that. No one would listen to him in servant's clothes. 'Well, I am wearing what I have on until we get to the port on Hand. Then maybe we can ask my mother for some of my clothes.'

'You would be a might smelly by then, and I really do not fancy sharing a cabin with you under those conditions. In fact, I have to say you are a little smelly already. The captain holds some clothes for me in times of need, he may have something that would fit you until you need to become a peacock on display.'

'Thank you,' Seamus said gratefully.

'And while I am finding out, you could perhaps take that frippery to Aliah.' He pointed to the pile of women's items on the table.

Pleased to be doing something, Seamus picked up the clothes along with a couple of books from their chest and took them down the hall to where Aliah's cabin was said to be. As he drew close, he heard laughter from within. He knocked on the door and was surprised to see it opened by Guard Daniel.

'Come in, come in ... Oops, maybe not. It is a little

tight for space in here with the mess Aliah has created.' He shuffled around to try and make room for Seamus. 'Perhaps it is best if I come out so you may come in.'

'No, it is all right,' Seamus mumbled. 'I just came to drop these off for Aliah.'

'And no doubt pick up some of what she has just pulled from her chest. We were just discussing what would happen if she arrived at your father's court wearing some of this. It was obviously meant for you.' Daniel smiled. 'I have to check in with the captain, then have a talk with a new recruit I seem to have acquired. I can only imagine how Dominic feels his new position in my guard will work, and I need to talk to him before some of those ideas take hold. So you can keep Aliah company in my absence. Maybe persuade her to actually clean up after herself because there is no one else to do it.' Daniel moved out of the room to make space for Seamus then shut the door behind him.

'I did not mean to cut his visit short,' Seamus said, a little confused at the scene he had witnessed, and still not really comfortable being in Aliah's company.

Aliah looked up from her place on the floor beside the trunk. Clothes were strewn throughout the room, every surface covered in something.

'Daniel has work to do but it was nice to spend a little time with him. It was hard being at home like that and not getting to see all of my family. Daniel and I grew up together so he is like a big brother. We used to practice sword work until he joined the guards and it embarrassed him if I beat him.' Aliah's face softened fondly at the memory.

'I am sorry, it must have been hard for you yesterday. To finally arrive home and then to leave so quickly, not seeing your sister or even really getting to say good-bye to your father.'

'Mmm,' Aliah answered, her head in the trunk rummaging. When it popped out she said, 'But there is an improvement. This time, I am leaving as my father's representative to talk with a Head of State. Last time, I was being sent off to marry a barbarian. It is nice to be good for something other than getting married.' Her head ducked back into the trunk.

'Are you looking for something in particular?' he asked.

'I most certainly am. If I am to be stuck in this room until Port Isby they could have at least given me something to pass the time.'

'You mean some embroidery perhaps?' Seamus said, then ducked the shoe Aliah threw at him. 'Or maybe these?' He held up the three books he had in his hand, bound with a note from Aliah's father. The note read, 'If you are going to represent me it is about time you read some of our history written by earlier statesmen.'

'Ahh, he is so frustrating!' Aliah exclaimed.

'What do you mean?'

'Well, take these trunks with clothing that just happen to fit the both of us. I think it is likely he had them packed while he was talking with Dominic and Walter. And the fact that there are books on the history between Hand and Aria? I thought when he was presenting our options that he was doing it in a way that led us to choose what he wanted us to do. I believe he never had any intention of sending me away, in fact he planned for you and I to

BEGINNINGS

both represent him all along. This note just proves it.'

Aliah flopped down on the one chair ignoring the clothing it was covered with.

'He knew you would come rather than be married off to some stranger, but he cannot have known I would agree to his plan,' Seamus said.

'Really? Walter knew you were no longer keen on studying at the Wizard Isles. Could you really have gone to some foreign land while a war raged through Aria? I think not, and Walter would have known that too. This option gives you an opportunity to spend time with your family again, even if you do not get to stay. I would have bet on your going ... so did he.'

'The crafty old ...'

'Careful. That is the king and my father you are talking about.' Aliah laughed, and he joined her.

'Are you happy to be going home?' Aliah finally asked him.

'It will be good to see my mother, my father too I guess. But I really have no idea how my father will react to my having magic. He could just as soon banish me or have me held in the dungeons as welcome me home.'

'Maybe it is as your aunt said, he is not as strict about the old ways as he seems. You should trust him to find a solution.'

'Maybe. But at least it will be out in the open. And I have a little protection being on your father's business, so my father with think twice about doing anything rash when he sees me. I guess the king thought of that as well.' Seamus surprised himself at how relieved he was to have the opportunity to see his parents again. Being away from them made him realise how much he missed them, and to not have them in his life at all would be hard.

'And it is kind of nice to be travelling home in luxury feeling safe again, even if it is only for a while.'

Aliah found a small area not covered in clothing and indicated he should sit. 'My last experience was not so different to this though. I will still be stuck in a cabin unable to see what all the fuss over sailing the seas is about.' Clearly she did not have fond memories of her first trip.

As if suddenly struck by a thought Aliah looked at him. 'Are you all right with this. I mean working with me really. You know ... after ...'

'After you left me without a word and headed out on your own,' he finished for her.

Aliah wriggled in discomfort. 'Well, yes.'

Seamus looked her in the eye. 'I really am all right with it. It seems the fates want us to be together for the moment, and you have shown me you are not so likely to act without consideration again. And if you do decide to go off on a tangent, I am at least prepared for it this time.' Seamus was almost as surprised as she was at the words that came out of his mouth. As he uttered them he realised he really was no longer angry with her.

'Shall we sort through these things and see what needs to go in my trunk. Then maybe I can find some cards or a set of Last Man Standing. There is nothing to say that you have to be stuck here alone. And there is always your father's books.' He smiled. 'Then after we leave Port Isby you will be allowed on deck and maybe we could continue with developing our hand to hand combat techniques. I would love to try actually using them to fight."

Aliah returned his smile. 'This trip will definitely be better than the last! We will make it so because we have seen that together, there is nothing we cannot do.'

'Aliah?'

'Mmm.'

'I spoke with Walter last night. Wizard Millard could not find a trace of magic in me. He thinks this means I am either a really strong wizard, or that Millard was playing games.'

'Now that is interesting.' Aliah looked closely at him. 'Which do you think it is?'

Seamus paused and watched her put away some of her clothing into the trunk. 'I don't really know. You don't suppose that what Pauley said about us being The Wizard and The Warrior from the prophecy could be true do you?'

Aliah spluttered in a very unladylike way. 'No, silly. Those old men would not have written a prophecy about a woman warrior, and though you can fight I would not describe you as a warrior. And although you can make a tiny flame no one in their right mind would call you a wizard.'

'I guess you are right.' Seamus agreed, but in his head he wondered if maybe he and Aliah had less control over the events that had brought them to this point than they imagined. He shrugged his shoulders, only time would tell. For now he had best help Aliah sort out the mess that was her room.

ABOUT THE AUTHOR

Vivienne has been writing books since she was fifteen years old, but only friends and family were allowed to read them. Forced to give up work because of family commitments she was encouraged by friends and family to finally put some of her writing out there for others to read.

In the real world after leaving university with a BA in History and Politics she worked as a Personnel Officer, an Office Manager, a Project Manager, a DBA and IT Manager then as a Business and Data Analyst, adding an MSC in Information Systems along the way. In her world she continued to write.

Born in Invercargill (New Zealand), she has lived in; Dunedin (New Zealand), London (England), Petersfield (England) and currently lives with her husband and son and their dog Trouble and kitten Lola in Sydney (Australia).

For future releases and current news you can find Vivienne at **www.viviennelfraser.com.au** or on Facebook at **www.facebook.com/vivienneleefraser**

ACKNOWLEDGEMENTS

This book has been years in the making and as I have written it I realise that, just like for raising children, it takes a village to produce a book.

None of this would have been possible without the support of my husband Jim, or the beta reading and incessant questioning of my son Sam (who the book was written for).

I also want to thank my mum Barbara and my aunt Avis for their proof-reading skills (all for a bottle of wine!), and thank you to their parents for raising children who believe grammar is an essential part of life.

Thank you to my editor, Heather Bosevski. I did not even know I needed you, but you took my story and developed it into something way beyond what I expected to achieve.

The publishing of this book would not have been so easy without the help of K. A. Last, who was happy to share her self publishing knowledge and experience, and really this book would not be what it is without her. She also designed the amazing cover and set the book out for me. You can find her books at www.kalastbooks.com.au.

I want to thank all those friends and family over the years who have read my books and stories and encouraged me to do this. And finally to all those who have read this book—I hope you enjoyed it and welcome to my reading family.

You can keep up with Wizard and Warrior news
on Facebook @wizardandwarrior